WITCHES & WORDS

A LIBRARY WITCH MYSTERY

ELLE ADAMS

Fireworks exploded across the midnight sky, to the sound of cheering from the crowd gathering on the seafront. Even the persistent drizzle couldn't dampen our spirits, and neither could the high tide, lapping at the edges of the pier and the walkway bordering the beach.

My cousin Estelle and I stood among the crowd on the walkway, watching the shower of sparks merge into the image of a shimmering unicorn etched against the night sky.

"I bet that's giving Cass ideas," I remarked as the unicorn broke into a gallop across the starry backdrop. Estelle's sister stood closer to the beach than the two of us, with Aunt Adelaide keeping one eye on her to make sure she stayed out of trouble.

"Happy New Year!" cried a few hundred voices, followed by more cheering.

Estelle and I wore thick layers beneath our bibliowitch uniform—black cloaks decorated with the silver emblem unique to our family and hats crammed on top of our curly red hair—but the chill found its way into my cloak all the same. The two of us looked similar enough to be mistaken for sisters, though Estelle had inherited her curvier figure from her mother, while I had Mum's willowy figure and Dad's paler face and freckles.

Next to us stood Alice, who worked in the pet shop, and Zee, who owned the bakery and had brought a bag of cookies and other delicious baked goods. We munched companionably as we watched the fireworks, a magical barrier protecting us from the spray of the sea crashing against the sand. Two more unicorns joined the first, galloping beneath the crescent moon until they reached the place where the sea and the sky became one.

"They say you have to make a wish when the first star of the new year appears," Estelle said into my ear.

"The first *falling* star," Zee corrected. "It doesn't happen every year, but you have to say your wish aloud, or else it won't come true."

"Exactly," said Alice. "Reckon we'll get lucky this year?"

Estelle nudged me. "We might."

The fireworks masked all the stars from view, but my good mood faded a little as I considered I might wish for.

I had so many reasons to be grateful. A year ago, I'd been stuck working the New Year's Eve shift at the bookshop where I'd been an assistant for the three years following my dad's death. My boss, Abe—who would have opened the shop on Christmas Day if he could get away with it—had ordered me to arrive first thing in the morning to pick up a delivery, so I hadn't even stayed up until midnight to see the new year in.

If I'd travelled back in time to that day to tell my past

self that within a few short months, I'd learn that I was part of a family of biblio-witches who had a gift for making words come to life, I'd never have believed it. Let alone that I'd lose that awful job and move to my family's enchanted library in the coastal town of Ivory Beach. Not only did I have a new family and home, I even had a wand of my own—my dad's old wand, no less, which he'd left behind when he'd moved away from the magical world to marry my mum.

Life was almost perfect... except for one thing. No matter how many times I tried to banish his image from my mind, I couldn't forget that a few weeks ago, I had been dating—or thought I'd been dating—Xavier, until he'd left town without so much as a message or call. All I'd found was a note from his boss, consisting of a couple of terse sentences: *We have left town. Do not contact my apprentice again.*

I'd always figured that the Grim Reaper's apprentice dating a human wasn't common, but Xavier had never acted like it was a big deal. That he'd just taken off with no explanation had left me feeling wrong-footed and confused, even though I was the one who'd caught the Grim Reaper's attention by refusing to walk out of Xavier's life in the first place. Forbidding me from having a relationship with his apprentice was the least of what the angel of death could do to me, I knew, but that didn't make it hurt any less.

Aunt Candace hadn't helped matters, with her constant hints that our ill-fated relationship would provide the perfect plotline for a tragic love story. It wasn't out of the ordinary for my aunt to take real-life inspiration for the novels she penned, but when she'd brought her notebook to the table at Christmas dinner, Aunt Adelaide had threatened to turn it into a Yorkshire pudding. Being mentioned in the dedication of the novel based on my dad's life story—though not by name—was quite enough publicity for me, thanks.

I pushed the thought away and smiled up at the firework display above, now dominated with a dozen unicorns wheeling across the darkness. Unicorns were a good omen, right?

Estelle tugged on my elbow. "My mum wants us."

"Why?"

"I don't know."

The two of us edged out of the crowd towards where Aunt Adelaide stood on the road behind the beach. At her side stood a tall man wearing a long dark coat that blended into the surrounding darkness, a hood obscuring his face.

"This man wants access to the library," said Aunt Adelaide. "I wouldn't ask either of you to volunteer, but I think Candace must have used an earplug charm to block out the fireworks."

That didn't surprise me. Aunt Candace had refused to come and stand in the cold and had instead opted to stay in the library and work on her novel. The library was supposed to be closed until noon tomorrow, so there must be some special reason this guy wanted to get inside. I squinted at the stranger, trying to make out his features. He wore a long, hooded coat buttoned to his chin, which wasn't that unusual, considering the weather, but made it hard to make out anything about him apart from his height.

"I need to get to the library and return a book," he said,

his voice low and raspy. "Can one of you help me out? It's urgent."

Estelle looked as perplexed as I felt. "Urgent?"

Returning a book wasn't generally a life or death matter. Okay, the head of late fees was Sylvester, our temperamental talking owl familiar, but even he'd taken the night off.

The man turned to Aunt Adelaide, and said in a low voice, "It's a time-sensitive loan."

Aunt Adelaide's brows rose. "Is that so?"

"Yes," he said, his voice solemn.

"What's that mean?" I whispered to Estelle.

"Time-sensitive?" said Estelle. "Some books get a little restless when they aren't returned on time… oh, no."

"What—?" I broke off, following her gaze. Cass's red hair shone in the moonlight as she waded into the ocean, her dark cloak billowing behind her in the water.

Aunt Adelaide swore. "I'll get her out of there. One of you can handle this gentleman's request, can't you?"

Estelle opened her mouth to volunteer, but I stepped in. "I'll do it. I don't want you to miss the start of the year."

If I had to admit it, I had another motive: if a falling star made an appearance, I didn't want anyone to hear me voice my wish aloud, even my family and friends.

"If you're sure," she said. "Ask Sylvester to help you find the right section. He'll grumble at being disturbed, but he understands time-sensitive deadlines. Just make sure the book ends up where it's supposed to be before time runs out. How long do we have?"

"Twenty minutes," said the man. "Thank you."

"No problem." I waved goodbye to my cousin and walked with the hooded stranger towards the towering shape of the library dominating the town square behind the clock tower.

The library never failed to steal my breath away, especially lit up with lanterns as it was at night. Its stained-glass windows shimmered under the light of the fireworks, and inside were five stories of towering shelves arranged like a layered wedding cake, along with countless doors and staircases and secret passageways. A staircase off the left-hand side of the lobby led into my family's living quarters, while the shelves immediately behind the front desk contained lists of where all the books were to be shelved, and instructions for dealing with the particularly dangerous ones.

If the hooded stranger was impressed by the library, he didn't say so. There was no sign of Aunt Candace, nor Sylvester. I had no idea what the owl did with his free time, but he'd be annoyed at me for dragging him out of sleep to deal with a book when he'd been promised the night off. I'd start by calling my own familiar.

"Hey, Jet," I called. "I need your help."

"Hello, partner!" cried Jet. The little crow swooped down to land on the desk, his glossy black wings gleaming in the light of the floating lanterns above our heads.

I turned to the hooded figure beside me. "Where's the book I need to return?"

"Here." He reached into one of the deep pockets of his coat. "It's still early enough to make the deadline."

"Just about," said a bored-sounding voice from his pocket. "Get on with it, numbskull."

I startled. After living in the library for a month, I'd *almost* learned to stop jumping when random voices came out of thin air, but when the wizard pulled a thick leather-bound book from the pocket of his hooded cloak, my mouth fell open.

"Quiet," he said to the book. "I told you I was returning you on time."

"You're cutting it close," said the voice, which without a doubt came from the book itself. "It's almost midnight."

"The book talks to you?" I said.

"Isn't it annoying?" he said. "It's fixed with a sentience spell and jinxed to start wailing if it's returned late. The rest of the time, it chatters away like it'll shrivel up and vanish if it isn't the centre of attention."

"You talk all the time and nobody's trying to lock *you* up," growled the book. "Bloody hypocrites. Hey—let me go!"

The wizard held the book out to me, and I braced myself for it to bite or burn me or sprout wings and fly off —all of which I'd experienced at least once in the last month. When you worked in a magical library, you learned not to question the impossible. But I'd never met a book that talked back before. Thankfully, the book's bark seemed to be worse than its bite, because it didn't move an inch when I took it in my hands.

"Thank you," said the man. "Thank you so much."

"Don't think anything of it." I laid the book on the desk, wincing when it gave a loud, derisive laugh. "Jet, can you help me find the right section?"

The little crow flew down to land on the desk beside me. "Of course, partner!"

"Wait, you're leaving me here with that inexperienced little witchling?" said the book. "It's an outrage!"

Just my luck to get the book nobody else wanted to deal with. Jet flew in circles above the book while I consulted the long roll of paper on the desk to see which floor I needed. "Third floor... okay. We're going up."

Since Sylvester hadn't deigned to show his face, I picked up the book and tucked it under my arm. The book didn't like that a bit. "How dare you place your hands on me, witchling! I'm older than you are, and I deserve respect."

"I'm just doing my job," I muttered. "If you don't like it, it's not my problem."

"Talking to inanimate objects is the first sign of madness."

The book kept up a steady stream of complaints all the way through the lobby to the spiralling staircase. Already regretting volunteering to shelve it, I used my wand to cast a light spell—the first spell I'd asked Estelle to teach me after I'd acquired my wand—to illuminate the stairs. Then I began to climb.

When I reached the third floor, I lifted the book to my wand's light to read the number on the spine and found nothing but an unfamiliar symbol. Frowning, I turned it over to look at the front. More symbols filled the space where the title was supposed to be.

A sudden rush of suspicion zipped through me. This wasn't the first time I'd encountered a book containing an unreadable magical code. In fact, I had another in my bag right now—the journal my dad had kept before his death, which neither I nor my family had ever figured out how to translate. I couldn't tell for sure if it was the same code or just a similar one, but alarm bells started ringing in my head at the sight of the symbols on the cover.

"What're you staring at?" said the book.

"You're speaking English," I commented. "Yet your cover isn't written in any language I know."

"I couldn't get very far by speaking in Ancient Hebrew, could I?"

"*Can* you speak Ancient Hebrew?" I eased open the book, which slammed closed on my fingers. I gave a startled yelp and yanked my hand free. Ow.

"Keep your nose out or I'll bite that next," the book said.

I shook my throbbing hand. "That wasn't necessary. What language is that on your cover?"

"How should I know? I can't read."

Honestly. "Is your owner a vampire?"

"None of your business."

On the day of my introduction to the paranormal world, three vampires had barged into the bookshop where I worked in search of Dad's old journal. While my aunts had scared them off and one was now in jail, the other two vampires were still at large. My aunt's ex, Dominic, had mentioned that the three were members of a society who searched for lost artefacts, and for some reason, my dad's journal was on their list. I'd been doing my best to put the vampires out of mind, but the familiarity of that symbol on the book's cover was difficult to ignore.

"Are you going to shelve me or not?" asked the book. "Because I'm going to start screaming after ten past twelve, and it's already five minutes to midnight."

"Are you dangerous?" I asked.

The book laughed nastily. "It's a little late for you to be asking that question."

Oh, wonderful. "If you mean me harm, I can dispose of you."

"You'd destroy the property of your own library?"

Okay. Maybe I'm just being paranoid. Sure, the book kept yapping and biting my fingers, but that didn't mean it was evil. My aunt wouldn't have let it into the library if it were likely to cause any of us harm. Granted, it wouldn't share sensitive information about its own content, but the same could be said of most books beyond my novice level, and I could always ask Aunt Adelaide later. I'd shelve it, wash my hands of the problem and go back to celebrating the new year.

I flipped the book over to check the back cover, and the entire book turned inside out, revealing blank yellowed pages on both sides.

"Hey!" I said. "I need to know where to put you. I can't do that if I can't read your spine."

"Where to put me?" the book echoed. "You can put me down, for a start."

"Nice try, but I bet you'll start screaming if I put you anywhere other than your proper place when the deadline hits." I walked past the Magical Creatures Division in the hope of finding a signpost marking the 'Annoying Talking Books Division'. The books on the shelves broke into a chorus of snarls as I passed by, and the book in my hands growled back at them.

"Glad you're making friends," I said to the book, walking on towards a number of rooms marked with X symbols. I wouldn't learn to deal with those until I reached the next stage of my biblio-witch training, and if this particular book needed to be placed in one of them, I'd just call in Sylvester to help me. Not that I wanted to witness an argument between the book and the owl—though Sylvester was possibly the only person here who *could* out-argue a talking book.

I halted at the end of a row of doors. These ones weren't marked with X symbols, but instead bore marks which looked similar to the symbol on the book's spine. Now this was more like it.

"You're painfully slow," said the book. "I'd like to reach my destination sometime this century."

"All right, no need to be rude." I checked the book's spine again, and my gaze snagged on a door on my right, which was marked with the same symbol as the book. *There it is.*

I pulled out my Biblio-Witch Inventory and opened it, revealing the words I'd learned to infuse with magic. Tapping the word *open* with my fingertip, I braced myself and focused on the door. The wooden door sprang open and I held up the book as a shield, but there didn't appear to be anything inside the room except a single wooden table. I didn't blame my aunts for putting the book in isolation, considering its argumentative nature. A relieved breath escaped when I stepped into the room and left the book on the table without anything jumping out and biting me.

"Well, it's been fun getting to know you," I told the book. "Have fun in here."

"Wait," said the book. "Hang on. It's awfully dark in here, isn't it? Waaaaiiit…"

I closed the door and locked it, dusting off my hands with satisfaction and making a mental note to warn my aunts not to open that door without using an earplug charm first. For now, I checked the time. Almost midnight. I'd have to run if I wanted to make it back outside before the clocks struck twelve.

I took the stairs two at a time—skipping the ones that tended to vanish without warning—and ran through the dusty stacks of the ground floor. Then I skirted the front desk, pushed the oak doors open and halted on the doorstep, my eyes on the clock tower as it struck midnight.

Loud cheers rose from the crowd near the beach, audible across the town square in the lull between fireworks. In the velvet sky, a bright shape stood out among the surrounding stars, dazzling enough to draw the eye. Estelle was right.

The star detached itself from its fellow sparkling lights and tumbled towards the sea before winking out of existence. A small selfish wish rose, expanding inside my chest as the first fireworks of the new year exploded across the sky.

Speaking quietly, I voiced my wish aloud, following the barely visible trail of the star with my eyes.

As the clock tower chimed midnight, I wished for Xavier to come back.

I'd planned to sleep in late on the first day of the new year, but Sylvester woke me by singing 'Auld Lang Syne' in my ear at full volume.

"Hey!" I sat bolt upright in bed. "You know we're not open until noon, don't you?"

"I'm bored," said the owl, landing on my bedpost in a flutter of tawny wings.

I yawned. "You're bored? Go and annoy someone else. Aunt Adelaide always gets up early."

So did Estelle. Aunt Candace and I were not morning people, as Sylvester knew well. Unlike most owls, he rose early and slept at night, which was one of many small clues that he was no ordinary bird. Considering he had the entirety of the library's knowledge at his beck and call, you'd think he'd have more interesting hobbies than trying his level best to annoy me.

"You talk in your sleep," said the owl. "You sounded rather miserable, so I thought I was doing you a kindness by waking you up."

"I did?" Please tell me I hadn't been dreaming about Xavier again.

The owl sprawled dramatically on my pillow. "Oh, Reaper. Don't leave me, Reaper."

My face flushed crimson. "Shut up."

Sylvester hooted with laughter. "Reeeaaaper!"

"Quiet," I snapped. "If you don't want me to give away your big secret, you're not to repeat any of that again to anyone, including my family members. Is that clear?"

He hopped into an upright position and fluffed his feathers. "There's no need for that, Aurora."

I shooed Sylvester out of my room, then I showered and dressed, trying to reboot my brain to optimism mode. Dreams notwithstanding, I would *not* be starting the year off by lamenting what I couldn't have. After all, I had three hundred and sixty-five days of a new year ahead of me and I planned to make the most of every single one of them. If I had it my way, my first full year in the library would be one to remember.

My phone buzzed as I left my room with a message from my best friend, Laney, wishing me a happy new year. Laney was my one remaining friend from my life before I'd moved to the library and had no idea the magical world existed, due to the strict rules forbidding me from sharing the existence of the paranormal with any non-paranormal. I had mixed feelings on said rules, which were the reason it'd taken twenty-five years and a brush with death at the hands of a group of vampires for me to learn I had a whole other family I'd never met. I dashed off a response to Laney, hoping the message didn't take two days to reach her this time, and went downstairs.

To my surprise, I found Cass sitting alone in the living room. Maybe she couldn't sleep, either.

"Why do you look so miserable?" said Cass. "Don't tell me you're still moping over the Reaper. What did you expect when you invited him to a party?"

"I didn't invite him. He just showed up." I left the room and headed to the kitchen in search of coffee. "Besides, if I look miserable, it's because Sylvester woke me up early for no reason. Why doesn't he sleep during the day, anyway?"

"I imagine he keeps the same sleeping hours we do because it gives him more hours to annoy us," said Estelle from the kitchen. "The good news is, my mum left us breakfast, and since we're both awake, we can go and practise spells with your new wand."

"I like the sound of that." I walked in the kitchen and found someone had already set out plates of toast and mugs of coffee. I picked one up and inhaled the delicious smell of coffee grounds. One year I might try to kick the caffeine habit, but it wouldn't be this one.

"You're seriously excited about doing extra work?" Cass said from behind me.

"Hey, all my lessons have been on hold since Christmas Eve." I sat down and dug into my toast and jam.

Now I had my dad's old wand, I'd finally be able to start learning how to use it. And as Cass had caustically noted, I *liked* learning and practising magic. Cass didn't seem to like anything except the magical creatures she took care of.

On cue, she said, "I'm off to the third floor. Have fun with your schoolwork."

"Wonder which animal she'll bring in this year?" I said

to Estelle when she'd left. "Probably a chimera."

"Don't give her ideas," said Estelle. "The boggart and the minotaur were bad enough. And the kelpie. He came to the beach last night because he was freaked out by the fireworks, so she decided to go for a swim with him."

"I figured." I sipped my coffee. "Did Aunt Adelaide have to fish her out of the sea again?"

"Pretty much." Estelle took her plate to the sink. "To be honest, I think she swam out there so none of us would hear her saying her wish aloud. You know, the first wish of the year. You saw the falling star from the library, right?"

"I did, but I didn't think it would be Cass's thing," I said. "She isn't the whimsical sort."

"No, she isn't," said Estelle. "But Cass does like to keep things to herself. What did you wish, then? I won't tell." She winked at me.

My face heated. "I don't know if it counts if what you wish for is impossible. Even magic can't work miracles."

"You never know what might happen." Estelle gave me a sympathetic smile, as though she'd guessed the direction of my thoughts.

"I guess not." I took another sip of coffee. "It won't take me as long to get through the next round of magical exams now I have a wand, right?"

Estelle was a natural-born teacher and she enjoyed having a new pupil to work with, even an absolute newbie who'd crashed into the magical world by accident. It was a step down from working with undergraduates like she normally did, but Estelle had been nothing but patient with me.

"I doubt you'll have any trouble," she said. "You'll get

through the Grade Two exams easily enough. You just need to learn some basic potion-making. And then in the Grade Three exam, you'll need one 'extra' skill. I think familiar training will work perfectly. You and Jet are already doing well, so that shouldn't be an issue for you."

"And there's a theory test at each round, right?" I was lucky Estelle didn't make fun of me for reading my schoolbooks over the holidays. I'd got used to being the weird bookish outcast when I was a kid, but who wouldn't want to learn everything about the paranormal world? Magic might not be novel to Cass, but it was to me.

"There is," said Estelle. "You'll have separate theory and practical exams. We used to do both at the same time, but thanks to Cass, my mum banned pens and paper from the practical magic exams, after she kept using biblio-witch magic to cheat because she couldn't use a basic levitation spell. Don't tell her I told you that."

"Ha." I smiled. "I'm guessing she got the hang of it eventually."

"Not without a huge fuss," she said. "This *is* Cass we're talking about, after all."

"What's she done now?" said Aunt Adelaide, poking her head into the kitchen.

"Nothing yet, but she has a whole new year in which to get up to mischief," said Estelle. "Where's Aunt Candace?"

"Sleeping in, I imagine," she said. "Or fishing for rumours to give her a head-start on her next book."

"Oh, so that's where Jet disappeared to." My familiar liked catching up on the town's latest gossip, and Aunt Candace was the only person willing to listen to him for an extended length of time. Mostly because his chattering about the neighbours' lives gave her endless material for her books. "Guess some people had a wild night out."

Not me. I'd gone back to join the others on the beach until the fireworks finished and then retired to bed early. Estelle had stayed out longer, but she was always perky and wide-awake no matter how little sleep she'd had.

"I didn't see anything too outrageous," said Estelle. "A few people went swimming at midnight and had to be levitated out of the ocean before the tide swept them away."

"Happens every year, the fools." Aunt Adelaide retreated from the room. "I'm sorting this year's paperwork until we open. Give me a shout if you need me, okay?"

"Sure thing," said Estelle. "There aren't any other books that need returning, I don't think. Oh yeah, you did manage to return that book on time yesterday, Rory? I never asked."

I finished my coffee. "I've never had a book strike up that much of an argument with me before."

Estelle frowned. "The book talked to you?"

I put down my mug. "It didn't just talk to me, it turned itself inside-out to stop me from shelving it in the right section."

She grimaced. "Oh, no. I should have dealt with it instead."

"Nah, it would have been fine if I'd shelved it before the guy in the cloak disappeared," I said. "As soon as he was gone, the book started giving me grief. It probably knew I was a newbie and assumed it didn't have to show me any respect."

"Some of those old tomes get restless," she said. "You could have left it on the desk to sort out later."

"It would have started screaming if I'd been late putting it in the right place, so I reckon I got off easy." I shuddered. "What kind of book was it, anyway? It bit my fingers when I tried to open it and look inside, and the text on the cover wasn't written in English."

"Ouch," she said. "I have no idea, actually. I haven't dealt with a time-sensitive book for a while."

"That explains why there was nothing else in the room where I had to take it," I said. "It gave me a weird vibe, come to that. Should I not have gone in there alone?"

"If the room was empty, it's fine," she said. "Sylvester would have taken over if it'd been beyond your level."

"I didn't ask him for help because I figured he and the book would get into an argument," I admitted. "Let's just say the book made even Sylvester look polite, and that's saying a lot."

"Oh, boy." She waved her wand, and our plates and mugs levitated over to the sink. "All right, let's put that new wand of yours to use."

Since the library wouldn't open to the public until later, we opted to practise in the Reading Corner, a cosy area at the back of the ground floor filled with bean bags, hammocks and comfy chairs.

"Here will do," said Estelle. "We won't use any spells that might damage anything, but the library is used to students practising magic in the classrooms."

I pulled out my wand, anticipation building within me. While the long stick of wood looked the same as any other wand, the rush of energy that tingled through my palm when I held it was unmatched by anything except for my Biblio-Witch Inventory. I'd spent a few weeks practising basic wand movements ready to put them into practice, but my wand classes with my aunts weren't set to begin until later this week. If Aunt Candace's approach to practical lessons was anything like her theory classes, though, I'd be left to my own devices. Luckily, I'd always been a fast learner.

"Which spell do you want to start with?" Estelle asked.

"Uh… good question." I'd gathered quite a few words in my Biblio-Witch Inventory by now, including spells for levitating books, unlocking and locking doors, and all the other vital skills necessary for navigating a magical library. Memorising words came more naturally to me than complex wand movements, but I'd already mastered the light spell and I had no doubt I'd get used to my wand with practise. "I guess conjuring and levitation spells will be the most useful on the job. Is conjuring too advanced?"

"For you? No." Estelle lifted her own wand. "You shouldn't have any trouble envisioning a particular book and summoning it. It's not that different from the way you use biblio-witch magic."

"Only if the books don't talk back to me."

She grinned. "Don't worry, they won't, as long as you don't summon the one you put in that room."

"Believe me, I don't plan on ever setting eyes on it again." I faced the towering shelves and pictured a volume of poetry I'd picked up the other day. "Okay… let's try this."

I moved the wand in a complex zigzag pattern as I'd practised. There was a flash of light, and the book appeared in my hands.

"Perfect," said Estelle.

I lowered the book. "How do I send it back to where it came from?"

"Don't look at me." Sylvester flew over our heads, his huge feathery wings casting shadows on the carpet of the Reading Corner. "I'm not going to carry all the books you move around back to their shelves. I have better things to do than act as your carrier pigeon."

"If you hadn't appeared just then, we wouldn't have known you were around," I pointed out. "Anyway, you're the one who woke me up early in the first place."

"Practising spells, are you?" said Aunt Candace's voice from nearby. "Try not to break anything."

My other aunt stepped out from behind a bookcase. She was tall and thin with a wild nest of curly red hair which looked like it hadn't been brushed in several years. As usual, her pen and notebook floated in mid-air beside her, scribbling notes for her next project. It seemed she wouldn't be kicking the habit of spending most of her time hiding behind bookshelves eavesdropping on people. When she wasn't listening to Jet recount the town's gossip, that is.

"I'm sure you'd manage to get a good story out of it if I did." I crossed the Reading Corner to the shelf where the book belonged and slid it back into place. "Do conjuring spells get harder the further away your target is?"

"They do," said Estelle. "There's also a limit as to how far away you can go. Not outside the town's boundaries, I wouldn't think."

"Nonsense," said Aunt Candace. "The library would be bigger than the whole town if you laid out all the rooms side by side. Let's see if she can conjure something from the upper level."

"Even you can't conjure something if you don't know what it looks like," said Estelle. "Stop taunting her, Aunt Candace."

"I'm not taunting, I'm *challenging* her," said Aunt Candace. "She's the most powerful biblio-witch in a generation."

Heat crept up my neck. Only Aunt Candace could make that sentence sound like a taunt instead of a compliment. "Really?"

I was still a newbie to the world of magic, and as far as I was concerned, knowledge was power. The library contained much more of that than I did, and so did Sylvester, come to that. Sure enough, the owl let out a disapproving clucking sound. "Don't get big-headed. You can't hold a candle to Adelaide, and your grandmother could cast better spells with her eyes closed and her wand lying on the floor."

I rolled my eyes. "I'm not getting big-headed. Also, are you implying Grandma was more powerful than you?"

"Oh, even her skills were paltry compared to mine," the owl said, landing on a bookshelf and ruffling his feathers. "I am a superior being, after all."

"You're not a biblio-witch, you're an owl." *Or rather, you're the Book of Questions.* It was beyond me to figure out whether he was trying to taunt me into spilling his secrets to the others, or he was just being, well, Sylvester.

"And you're a—"

"Sylvester!" said Estelle. "Why do you stay here in the library if you think we're all stupid? Because we feed you?"

"*You* don't feed me," he said.

"That's because you only let Cass feed you," she said.

"The last time I tried, you bit my fingers and accused me of treating you like a common animal. I don't know why you make an exception for Cass."

"I humour her. She respects me, after all."

"Because she likes animals more than people." Estelle folded her arms. "And she's the one who cast the spell that made you talk. If not for us, you'd be flying around hooting and nobody would understand you."

Since I'd never known otherwise, it often slipped my mind that Sylvester hadn't always been able to talk. No wonder it'd taken so long for anyone to realise he was the living embodiment of the library's knowledge. Even I'd only worked it out by sheer luck, and it didn't make the owl any easier to figure out. I ignored his comments and returned to practising conjuring spells until Aunt Candace got bored and slipped away behind the shelves.

"Try conjuring *her*," said Sylvester, with a rather nasty cackle. "That'll wake her up."

"You're being particularly vindictive this year," I told him.

"It's only been one day," he said. "I'm just getting started."

Estelle pointed her wand at the owl. "Go on, stop hanging over us. I'm sure you can find something else to entertain yourself with. Like that book Rory put away yesterday."

I shuddered. "Don't even."

"A book?" said the owl. "I require more excitement."

"What did you expect from a library?" Estelle rolled her eyes at him. "You might have joined a circus instead if you wanted more wild, hair-raising action."

The owl let out an indignant hoot. "I have never been

so insulted in my life. Also, I don't have hair. I have *feathers!*"

He swooped off, forcing me to throw my arms over my head to avoid being clipped by one of his wings. "He and that talking book are a match made in hell. I'd better hope I don't have to open that door again, or the two of them will either conquer or destroy the universe."

Speaking of the book... I still hadn't told Aunt Adelaide about the odd similarities between the code on its cover and the text inside my dad's journal. Everyone had been too wrapped up in the celebrations last night, and I hadn't wanted to bring the mood down by mentioning secret codes or vampires. Besides, there were hundreds of books in the library which had been written in little-known languages. A book containing a code that looked vaguely similar to the one in my dad's journal wasn't worth panicking over.

"You're making me glad I *didn't* volunteer to deal with it." Estelle raised her wand. "All right, let's get back to practising conjuring spells."

Without Sylvester or Aunt Candace hanging over me, my focus improved considerably—and as a bonus, none of the books started talking back.

"We'll try unlocking and locking spells another time," Estelle said. "Those are easy to misfire, and we don't want to set anything from the high-security rooms loose in the library right before we open for the day."

"No, we really don't." I returned each of the books I'd conjured to its place on the shelf. "Maybe we can practise long-distance conjuring when Sylvester's in a better mood so he can fly off and return the books to their rightful places. I'm not sure where this one goes." I held up the last remaining book.

"By the reception desk," she said, taking the book from my hand. "I'm going to open the library now, so I'll put it back."

"Thanks," I said. "That was much more fun than listening to one of Aunt Candace's theory lectures."

A shrill noise came from inside the family's living quarters.

"Oh… that's the phone," said Estelle. "Would you mind answering? I have to check the sign on the door is off at noon, so people know the library's open."

"Sure, no problem."

Who'd be calling the library on the morning of New Year's Day? Everyone knew we weren't open until noon, and half the town was nursing hangovers, too. *Please don't let it be another talking book with a time limit on it.* Though at least if it was, the rest of my family was around to help me deal with it this time.

As I headed into the living room, the phone gave another shrill ring. Since nobody else was in the room, I picked it up and answered the call.

"Hello?" said a male voice.

"Hello. This is Aurora Hawthorn, at the library. Who is this?"

"It's Mr Spencer. The man who returned a book to the library last night."

Wait. It was the guy who'd returned the talking book? I almost didn't recognise his voice, since he spoke in an urgent whisper and I hadn't seen his face last night.

"Is something wrong?" I asked. "Please tell me you don't want me to fetch the book again."

"No," he said. "The book—it's—"

The call cut out. I held the phone to my ear for another instant, then tried calling him back. The phone cut out again. I dialled again, but the dial tone went on for a moment and then ended.

"Who was it?" Estelle entered the living room.

"The guy who returned that talking book last night, but I think he's having trouble with his phone signal. Or we are." I redialled again.

"Hello?" said a breathless female voice that definitely didn't belong to the man I'd spoken to. "Who is this?"

I frowned. "Aurora Hawthorn. Who is this?"

"This phone is… it's… what's his name?" I heard more voices in the background. "Spencer. Mr Spencer. I'm sorry, but he's dead. He had the phone in his hand when he fell downstairs. I think… what is it, Frederick?"

There was the sound of muffled voices and clattering, then the voice of Frederick, the owner of the town's main seafront hotel. "Who are you?"

"It's Aurora, from the library," I said. "What happened to—Mr Spencer, the guy who was calling me?"

"There was an accident. It seems he tripped downstairs. Why did he call you?"

My grip on the phone tightened. *He's dead?*

"He didn't say," I said. "He visited the library last night, and when he called today, he said he had something urgent to say. But I lost the connection before he could finish his sentence. Is he really…?"

"Yes," said Frederick. "He seems to have fallen… are you sure he didn't say what he was calling you for?"

"No. I'm sorry." What else could I say? I lowered the phone and turned to Estelle. "We have a problem."

3

"He's *dead?*" Estelle's eyes widened. "We just opened, so one of us will have to watch the desk. I'll tell my mum..."

"I'll head to the hotel," I offered. "It was me he spoke to, and I should go and explain before anyone comes here asking why we were the last people he called before he died."

"Fair point," she said. "Be careful, Rory, okay?"

"I will," I promised.

It'd be a fine start to the year if we got involved in yet another murder case, but last night's events took on a whole new meaning now the last person who'd checked out the talking book was dead. Not to mention he'd been trying to tell me something about the book when he'd died.

I hurried out of the library and crossed the silent town square. No signs of yesterday's festivities remained, few people were around, and almost all the shops were closed. The clock tower struck noon as I walked down the road to the seafront, where Frederick's hotel stood on my left-hand side.

Before I reached the door, I came to an abrupt halt. The entryway to the hotel was smothered in thick shadows, and within, I saw two things. One was the man who'd come to the library last night, and the other was the Reaper.

My entire body locked to the spot as a deep, intense shiver ran through my bones. The shadows resolved into the outline of a shimmering doorway in mid-air, and the man stepped through it, sending a torrent of icy air blasting into me. My limbs unfroze and I took a step back, my teeth chattering. *What* was *that?*

The door vanished and the shadows cleared, revealing the hotel's entryway looking the same as it always did. Except for two things: a sprawling body lying at the foot of the staircase in the lobby, and Xavier standing next to it, holding his scythe in both hands.

Xavier, the Grim Reaper's apprentice. I'd know his golden hair and aquamarine eyes anywhere. No other Reapers looked that distinctive. Granted, the only other one I'd met was the Grim Reaper, a fearsome figure who lurked in shadows and terrified the living daylights out of anyone who set eyes on him.

Speaking of shadows... had I just witnessed Mr Spencer pass onto the next world? I'd seen him step through a door, yet his body lay solid and unmoving at the foot of the stairs, and the shadowy door was nowhere in sight. All that remained behind was the tall blond Reaper, whose eyes widened at the sight of me.

"Rory? What are you doing here?"

"I could ask you the same question." The old hurt came

rushing back, momentarily overtaking my shock. He'd been gone for nearly two weeks—though it felt much longer—and he'd left without so much as a goodbye, as though our friendship had meant nothing at all. Why hadn't he told me he was back in town?

"I'm here for the usual reason." He lifted the scythe over his head to return it to the sheath on his back. "At least he died quickly."

"What did he tell you?" Despite my hurt, curiosity won out. "Before he passed on?"

His hands froze on the scythe. "You saw?"

"I saw the guy step through a door, yes." I rubbed my chilled hands together. "Was that the afterworld?"

Xavier lowered his arms. "Yes, it was. Why did you want to know what he said to me?"

"He called the library," I explained. "Before he died. I came here to see if I could find out why."

I had an inkling Xavier wouldn't be able to call him back through that door so easily, but why had I seen it at all? According to the Reaper's rulebook, mortals weren't supposed to be able to see the world beyond the realm of the living, where the Reapers escorted the souls they reaped into the next world.

Xavier's brows rose. "Rory, how do you always end up involved in these situations?"

"If you mean situations involving dead bodies, you tell me." I *had* wondered who would take the Reaper's place, but that didn't ease the shock of his return. My chest ached, as though a physical force had punched the air from my lungs.

Footsteps came from within the hotel, where Mr Spencer's body lay sprawled at the foot of the main staircase. The hood of his long cloak had slipped when he'd fallen, revealing an ordinary man with blond hair, maybe in his early forties. He didn't look distinctive in any manner, so it seemed odd that he'd wanted to hide his face. To keep from being recognised, perhaps. Several of the other guests milled around the lobby, talking in hushed whispers to Frederick, the hotel's owner. The kindly wizard wore a lopsided grey hat perched on his mat of brown hair.

"Who's out there?" Frederick looked over at us. "Oh—it's you, Reaper. Who are you talking to?"

"It's Aurora—Rory." I stepped into view. "Mr Spencer called me this morning about a book he returned to the library yesterday. He was on the phone to me when he…" I broke off, indicating his fallen body.

One of the guests spoke to Frederick, who nodded. "I'll get everyone out of their rooms and inform them. Can you do me a favour and knock on all the doors, Reaper? I think some of the guests may have over-indulged last night and didn't hear me calling them."

"Sure," said Xavier.

Since nobody told me otherwise, I followed Xavier into the lobby. Few people would be awake at this hour on New Year's Day under normal circumstances, but the thunder of footsteps above suggested most of the guests at the hotel had woken up at the sound of the furore downstairs.

Xavier and I rode the lift to the first floor and knocked on the first door. As we did so, a loud crash sounded from inside the room.

"Sorry," said a female voice. "Be out in a second."

A moment later, the door opened, revealing a young

woman with long dark hair and pale features. She wore jeans and a long-sleeved shirt and looked ordinary enough to pass as a normal, were it not for the wand in her left hand. A tall dark-haired man appeared behind her. He wore jeans that were muddy around the edges, a tough-looking jacket, and a shirt that stretched across his broad shoulders.

"I'm Blair," she said. "And this is Nathan."

"I'm Rory." I startled when a small black-furred shape brushed past my ankles.

"Sorry, that's my cat," said Blair. "My familiar. He's called Sky."

"Miaow," said the cat.

"Has he been in your room the whole time?" I asked. "I mean, Mr Spencer tripped downstairs, didn't he?"

There was a good reason none of my family members had chosen a cat as their familiar. Climbing staircases that moved was hazardous enough without adding felines into the equation.

The cat at my feet let out a hurt *miaow*, as though he resented the implication that he'd caused the man to trip and fall to his death.

"Sky was in our room," said Blair. "Trust me, we'd know if he left."

"Sorry, I just wondered," I said. "Did you see or hear anything at all?"

Like Death, for instance? The thought entered my mind, unbidden, bringing a chill to my arms. There seemed no reason for me to have seen what I had, and the fact that I'd viewed Xavier in his role as Reaper had spooked me easily as much as the body itself did.

"No," said Blair. "I woke up to the sound of raised

voices somewhere on this floor. Then a minute or two later, I heard a crashing noise."

"Voices?" I asked. "Mr Spencer's voice?"

"One of them might have been," said Blair. "I don't know who the second voice belonged to, though. I was half asleep. I didn't look outside until after the crash."

"Who was the last person to see him alive?" asked Xavier.

"That would be me, I believe," said a voice from behind the door next to Blair's and Nathan's room. It opened, and a tall, thin man walked out. His thick dark hair was laced with grey, putting him at around Mr Spencer's age, and his sharp green eyes raked over Xavier and me. "I saw him this morning."

"You did?" Out of the corner of my eye, Blair looked at him with an odd expression, a mixture of interest and wariness. "When? Do you know one another?"

"We've travelled together before," said the man. "I'm Henry Blake."

"You've travelled together?" I said. "Wait, does that mean he's not from Ivory Beach?"

Why, then, had he borrowed a book from our library?

"No," said the man. "I'm not sure where he's living at the moment. I came here from Birmingham."

"You came all the way here over the holidays to return a book to the library?" I said, nonplussed. "What are you, work colleagues?"

They couldn't be romantically involved, surely, because they had separate rooms. But it seemed a weird time of year to take a trip to the beach for the sole purpose of returning a book. Admittedly, since the book in question started screaming when it was returned late, perhaps they did have a good reason to schedule a last-minute trip, but still.

"Not exactly," said Mr Blake. "We once worked in the same area of business. I was travelling in the region and offered to meet up with him…"

Blair cleared her throat, and everyone looked at her. "Nothing. Carry on."

"…and we arrived here last night."

Right, of course. If they'd arrived any earlier, I imagined he would have returned the book sooner. It didn't make it any less odd that they'd arrived in town at night-time on the last day of the year, when they must have known the library would be closed—and now, less than twelve hours later, one of them had ended up dead.

"You arrived here last night," I repeated. "So he returned the book to the library—"

"How do *you* know about the book?" he said.

"Because I work there," I said. "I was on the phone to him when he—"

His eyes widened. "You were? What did you hear?"

"He started to speak, then the connection cut out," I said. "Any reason?"

"No, not at all," he said, a touch too quickly.

Blair fidgeted. "You sure about that?"

"I didn't hear anything except his voice and then a crash." I watched Mr Blake's face carefully. "When did you last see him alive?"

"This morning," he said. "I was under the impression he was going to take an early-morning walk. He was on his way downstairs, but he didn't say where he was going. Are you two coming?" He addressed Blair and Nathan.

"Ah, I need to find my shoes first," said Blair, ducking

back into her hotel room. "Sky, *why* did you knock over my suitcase?"

"Miaow," said the cat, rubbing against my ankles. Animals usually didn't flock to me the way they did to Cass, but Sky lay down on the floor with a clear indication that I should stroke him. Mr Blake, meanwhile, headed for the elevator and out of sight.

"Here," said Nathan from behind the door. "Your shoe was under the bed. I think Sky was sleeping in it."

"I forgot I used the other one to prop the window open."

There were a few more shuffling noises, then Blair hurried out of the room, pulling on her shoes as she did so.

"Miaow," said Sky, as though to say, *hurry up.*

Blair looked between me and her fluffy black cat. "Sky doesn't normally trust strangers, but he seems to like you."

Sky let me give him one last stroke, yawning. He had oddly coloured eyes—one grey, one blue—and a single white front paw. Then, at Nathan's prompting, he sauntered back into the hotel room to let them lock the door.

Blair finished adjusting her shoes. "Just so you know, that Mr Blake guy? He was lying."

I frowned. "How do you know?"

"My witch talent lets me tell if someone's being truthful or not," she explained. "Comes in handy sometimes."

"I bet it does." I'd never heard of that particular witch talent before. "What was he lying about, then?"

"I know he was lying about how he was travelling in the area and happened to run into Mr Spencer by coincidence, but I'm not sure which bit was a lie," she said. "He also lied when he said he didn't know what the other dude was doing when he left his room. I'll try to ask him more questions, but..." She broke off as Nathan cleared his throat. "We came here for sun, sand and sea, not murders, so I should probably stay out of this one."

"Well, there's sand and sea. Not much in the way of sunshine." I heard voices down the corridor as another group of guests left their rooms at Xavier's prompting. "Ah, I should go and catch up with my friend. We were told to make sure everyone gets downstairs to the lobby."

Blair and Nathan headed for the lift, while I went looking for Xavier. I wished I could speak to him alone, but now was not the time to have a serious conversation about the state of our relationship. Assuming we had one, that is.

"Is it true?" A small man with curly grey hair stopped beside me in the corridor. Despite the relatively early hour, he wore a neat suit and tie as though he was on his way to an important business meeting. "Is Mr Spencer really dead?"

"Yes," I said. "Did you know one another?"

"No, but we had an interesting conversation about antiques last night. I thought he might be a collector, like me."

"Everyone downstairs!" Frederick's voice drifted up from the lobby as a steady stream of guests headed for the elevators.

I met Xavier coming the other way. "How'd you knock on all those doors so quickly?"

"Reaper, remember?"

Right, of course. Reapers came equipped with an array of useful skills, including superhuman speed and the ability to walk through walls. You'd think I'd remember that, considering I'd seen him reap a man's soul earlier. "Speaking of which, if you can go into the afterlife at any given time, can you call a soul back into this world?"

"Back?" he echoed. "No. It's a one-way trip, for humans at least."

A chill settled somewhere deep in my bones. *Now* he was speaking like a Reaper—as though he wasn't part of the human race at all. It'd been a long shot, the notion of calling back Mr Spencer's soul to ask how he'd died, but if I believed Blair, it was Mr Blake who had something to hide. Perhaps the other man might be able to shed some light on why he'd called the library before his death. Whether his death had been accidental or otherwise, he'd been trying to tell me something important about that book, I was almost certain of it.

When Xavier and I reached the ground floor, we found the other guests milling around the lobby. Some looked barely awake after last night, while several appeared to still be drunk. Most of them were still wearing pyjamas or dressing gowns. A witch wearing fluffy dragon slippers and a lopsided hat lay sleeping against the reception desk, while a tipsy elderly witch held an animated conversation with the curly-haired collector.

"I've called Edwin," said Frederick. "Aurora, Reaper… you weren't witnesses, so you should leave before the police arrive."

"Do you think his death was an accident?" I asked him.

"I hope it was," he said. "But with no direct witnesses, it's anyone's guess. Edwin might want to hear what he said to you on the phone before he died."

"He didn't get the chance to say much," I told him. "He just said, 'the book'."

"What book?" said Xavier.

"The book he returned to the library last night." I felt my face heat under his stare. "You already reaped his soul. Why are you staying?"

"I'm not." He glanced around. "Might sound morbid, but this is the closest to normal I get."

I arched a brow. "Dealing with dead people?"

"Dealing with *people,*" he said. "Spending the holidays with the Grim Reaper is not the highlight of my year."

I pushed the door open and we escaped onto the seafront. "You didn't have to spend the holidays with him, did you?"

"Death never takes a day off, even Christmas," he said mildly.

"Then why did you leave town?" I asked. "Aren't you and your boss responsible for this entire region? I mean, you couldn't have known nobody in town would need the services of a Reaper over the holidays."

"I was still in the area," he replied. "My boss wanted me to go with him to… I suppose you might call it a conference for Reapers like me. I mentioned it, didn't I?"

"No." Since when did Reapers have conferences? I'd definitely have remembered him mention one, that was for sure. "Your boss told me never to contact you again. I assume this—" I gestured between the two of us—"doesn't count, since I didn't actually know I'd run into you today."

A shocked expression crossed his face. "My boss said that?"

"He did." The words of his message were burned into my brain by now. "He left a note in the library warning me to never to contact his apprentice again. Unless he has another apprentice who I didn't know about, that's you."

"Didn't you get *my* note?" he asked. "I told you I was going out of town for a few days, but I'd be back in the new year. It was a last-minute thing, so I dropped by your place during the night on my way out of town."

"You left a note?" My thoughts stuttered to a halt, my anger giving way to confusion. "I didn't find one."

"I put it on the front desk," he said. "I suppose the library needed tidying after that Manifestation Curse came to an end, so it might have gone missing somewhere."

"Maybe Sylvester or Cass hid it." Or perhaps the Grim Reaper himself had removed Xavier's note and left his own in his place. He'd made his feelings on our relationship pretty clear, after all. Yet the thought that Xavier *hadn't* known about the note made my mood brighten considerably.

"Maybe." He didn't look happy. "I'll have a word with my boss and see if he knows."

"Never mind," I said. "You're not getting yourself into trouble on my account again. Anyway, he'll be angry enough that I saw you escort that guy through the door into the afterworld, I imagine."

"I'm not telling him that," he said. "Mostly because I don't understand it myself. You're mortal, as far as I'm aware."

"I was the last time I checked." I took in a deep breath. "So… can you tell me what Mr Spencer said to you at the door, or whatever it was? I won't tell a soul."

"I would, but it's not repeatable in polite company. He

yelled obscenities at me until I managed to get him through into the next world."

"Oh." I frowned. "Is that common?"

"Surprisingly," he said. "Or perhaps not. Most people don't like being told they're deceased."

"It's hardly your fault he's dead," I said, with a rush of indignation on his behalf.

"No, but he might have thought I was someone else," said Xavier. "Believe me, I've heard worse. When they aren't cursing me, sometimes people think I can pass on messages to their loved ones."

"Can you?"

"Generally, no," he said. "I'm only the Reaper apprentice for this small region. It's not like I can pop over to the other side of the world to give messages to their distant relatives."

"I guess not," I said. "So you can't travel across the world in a second?"

"Theoretically?" he said. "Yes, I can. But finding individual souls gets tricky when there's distance involved. A lot of guesswork."

"Is that why you can't use a phone?" I queried.

"I can use one, but my boss and I are able to communicate without the need for technology." He looked at the clock tower. "I'd better go before he comes looking for me. I'm not leaving town, Rory, I promise. Talk later, okay?"

"Sure." I didn't know what else to say. My head was in a tailspin. Not only did Xavier want to see me again, he hadn't known his boss had left that note at all. He'd thought I'd known he was coming back.

Note to self: convince the Grim Reaper to let him get a

mobile phone. The level of control he had over his apprentice annoyed me at the best of times, but who was I to judge the Reaper by the same standards as the rest of us? He wasn't alive, for a start. At least, he didn't age, didn't need to eat or sleep, and could run for miles without tiring or walk out into the sea at high tide without taking a breath. And the Grim Reaper was responsible for all of those talents.

And you really thought you had the chance of a romantic relationship with him? I gave myself a mental shake when I looked up and realised he'd vanished from sight, moving at a speed no human could ever hope to achieve. If ever there was proof that I'd got caught up in a severe case of wishful thinking, that was it. Xavier was the Reaper, and the role fitted him like a glove. He'd never walk away from it for my sake. I *knew* that. But I couldn't stop the smile that stole onto my mouth at the idea that he'd been looking forward to seeing me after all.

I shoved the thought out of mind and continued on my path to the library. After the trouble that talking book had given me, the last thing I wanted was to unlock its room again, but I needed to at least tell my family before the rest of the town found out.

Besides, while I might never know why Mr Spencer had called the library, perhaps the book might shed some light on why someone might want to kill its owner.

4

Back in the library, I found my family members all assembled in the lobby. Judging by the unusually serious expression on her face, Estelle was explaining the situation to the others.

Aunt Adelaide turned to me as I walked in. "Is he really dead?"

"Are we supposed to care?" Cass wanted to know. "It sounds like he deliberately returned that book at the last minute to make trouble for us and then someone bumped him off."

"Whatever happened to being nicer this year?" said Estelle.

"Did I ever make that promise?" said Cass.

I rolled my eyes. "That would be too much to ask. Yes, he's dead. I still have no idea what he was trying to tell me on the phone before he died, but all he said was 'the book.'"

"Which book was it?" said Aunt Candace. "Why did nobody tell me about this?"

"You were hiding away from the fireworks last night," I said. "Mr Spencer showed up just before midnight with a book which needed to be returned within twenty minutes. If one of us hadn't returned the book to the library on time, it'd have started screaming. Now I'm starting to think I should have left it with him after all."

"Where is it?" Aunt Candace's pen and notebook hovered in the air expectantly, as they always did when something story-worthy happened.

"Really, Candace," said Aunt Adelaide. "It's up on the third floor. In an empty room, Estelle says."

"Yeah, there was nothing else in there," I said. "The guy he was with told me it was a long-term loan. When did he take it out?"

"We're checking the logbook. It might have been years ago," said Estelle. "Rory said the book wouldn't let her read it, Mum."

"It bit my fingers when I tried," I explained. "Then it turned inside-out when I tried to read the number on the spine. I got it into the room in the end, but... but the text on the cover and on the spine wasn't written in English. It was some kind of code, I think. Or another language."

I caught Aunt Adelaide's gaze, which flared with understanding. "A code?"

"We have books written in hundreds of codes and languages in here," said Aunt Candace. "You need to be a bit more specific if you want us to pinpoint the right one. I remember encountering one which was only readable when viewed through a particular pair of spectacles—"

"Yes, we know," interrupted Aunt Adelaide. "It's not unusual for clients to take out long-term loans on books that are particularly difficult to read."

"Is he part of a secret agency?" asked Aunt Candace. "Were they the ones who killed him?"

My aunt's pen scribbled so hard in her notebook that ink splattered everywhere.

"Candace!" said Aunt Adelaide. "You said he was travelling with someone, Rory?"

"Kind of." I relayed what Mr Blake had said, along with my suspicions that he wasn't being entirely truthful about how he and Mr Spencer had run into one another. "I assume Mr Spencer had a good reason for wanting a book that talks back and isn't nice about it."

Aunt Adelaide pursed her lips. "Like many of our rarer items, that book has various protective spells on it."

"But you still let him check it out and run off with it for months?" I frowned.

"I can't recall when it was." Her brow furrowed. "Perhaps if we find the record in the logbook, it'll prompt my memory… unless it was you who handled it, Candace?"

"Really, you can't expect me to remember every person who checks out a book from here," said Aunt Candace. "Especially long-term loans. I can't even remember who we dealt with last week, let alone a year ago."

"He was a guy wearing a long, hooded cloak," I said. "It would have stuck in my mind if I'd seen him before."

"Are there any collectors of dark mystical artefacts who *don't* wear hooded cloaks?" said Cass. "I thought it was part of the dress code."

"I wrote a book where they wear pink, just for variety," supplied Aunt Candace.

"Thank you for that contribution," Aunt Adelaide said. "Candace, if it was you who dealt with him, then you ought to have looked into his background before you handed him the book."

"I assume I did." Aunt Candace plucked her notebook and pen out of the air. "He wasn't that suspicious-looking, aside from the cloak, was he?"

"I didn't see him without the cloak until after he was dead, so I don't know," I said. "It was dark last night, even in the library. It's not that weird that he kept his hood up considering how cold it was, either. He didn't sound sinister at all. He just sounded like he wanted to get rid of the book."

"He's hardly the first secretive individual to visit the library," said Aunt Adelaide. "We tend to be careful when it comes to collectors of rare books, since so many of ours are one-of-a-kind. There would have been a background check involved, whoever dealt with him. I can't say anything stood out to me about his appearance that gave me any warning signs last night, either."

"Shouldn't there be a rule against loaning books to people who might want to steal them?" I asked.

Cass snorted. "You'd think so, but everyone here has more faith in the good of humanity than I do."

"You do realise the book is cursed to start screaming at full-volume if it isn't returned to the library on time?" said Aunt Candace. "There are other nasty curses on all our books which kick in if they're given away, or sold, or kept too long past their due dates. If I valued my life and sanity, I wouldn't want to check out a rare book from our library without carefully planning when to return it."

"Exactly," said Aunt Adelaide. "Besides, he must have taken the requirements seriously if he came here just before midnight on New Year's Eve. If he'd planned to keep the book for himself, he wouldn't have come back to Ivory Beach at all. Where does he live, do you know?"

"No idea," I said. "Maybe I should have asked Frederick, but he told me to leave before the police showed up."

"Yes, that was probably the best course of action," said Aunt Adelaide. "There's no obvious link between him and us… except for the book."

"Yeah." I looked down. "When he was on the phone, he sounded… scared, I think. He was whispering, as though he was afraid of being overheard. And even if his death was an accident, he wouldn't have called us for no reason."

"People think his death was an accident?" said Cass. "He was a lone traveller wearing a hooded cloak who returned a rare book to the library right before he died. Not one part of that isn't suspicious."

"He had friends," I said. "One of them was staying at the hotel. Mr Blake. He and Mr Spencer knew one another, and he admitted they argued this morning. He also said they used to travel together."

If Blair's lie-sensing powers were as accurate as she claimed, there was more to it than that. Unless it was Blair herself who was being less than truthful, but she'd have no obvious reason to deceive someone she'd never met before. The question was, what was Mr Blake trying to hide?

"Who else is staying at the hotel?" asked Aunt Adelaide.

"Uh, there was this woman, Blair Wilkes, and her boyfriend Nathan," I said. "They were here on holiday. There was also this older guy… he said he was a collector of some kind. He had a conversation with Mr Spencer about rare artefacts the night before, he said."

"Collector?" said Aunt Adelaide. "Of what?"

"I didn't get the chance to ask," I said. "Edwin showed up to talk to Frederick, so I had to leave before I got roped into the questioning. I came straight home."

"After talking to half the guests?" Cass gave me a suspicious look that implied she knew I hadn't told them everything, but I wasn't about to bring up the Reaper in front of her. Not until I'd had the chance to process his return.

"Frederick asked me to knock on their doors, since I was there," I said. "Everyone was sleeping off their hangovers. Almost everyone." The collector had seemed pretty alert compared to the rest of them, but I didn't know anything else about him.

"Was he a collector of rare books as well as other arte-facts?" said Aunt Candace. "Collectors would certainly be interested in getting their hands on some of our titles. It wouldn't be the first time one of them showed up in town."

"Are you forgetting Mr Spencer already returned the book to the library before he died?" said Estelle. "If anyone wanted the book, they'd have come here, not gone after him."

"They might not have known he'd already returned it," said Aunt Candace, undeterred.

"Don't be absurd," said her sister.

"She has a point," I said. "I mean, he slipped out at midnight wearing a cloak and hood and blended into the crowd celebrating the new year. If he ever brought it up in conversation, it's not like he'd have mentioned the exact time and date it was due back."

Unless the book had started yapping at him, that is. If I

were a collector of rare books, there must be something seriously special about that one to put up with its terrible attitude.

"No…" Aunt Adelaide paused. "I intend to speak with Frederick about his guests, once the police have finished their questioning. In the meantime, I think we'd better take another look at that book."

"Why bother?" said Cass. "We know what happened. Someone pushed him downstairs to steal a book he didn't even have. So, we double our security, leave the book alone, and the police will take care of the rest."

"Cass, you weren't even there," said Estelle. "That Mr Blake… did he seem suspicious in any way?"

"He admitted to arguing with Mr Spencer not long before he fell," I said. "I'd leave it up to the police, but I doubt Edwin wants to have a conversation with the book."

Neither did I, for that matter, but if the book was linked to Mr Spencer's death—and if he'd really been trying to give me a warning before he'd died—then it was better that we knew sooner rather than later. Whatever Cass said, the case wouldn't end with Mr Spencer's death, not if the book was the killer's target.

"All right," said Aunt Adelaide. "You lead the way, Rory. I admit I haven't been in that section for a while, so I might need a refresher."

"I remember the symbol, don't worry." After the last day's events, I wouldn't be forgetting that book for a long time. "It was near the very end of the back row of doors."

As Aunt Adelaide and I climbed the stairs, the sound of growling came from somewhere above our heads.

"Oh, no," she said. "Don't tell me Cass left the door to the Magical Creatures Division open again."

"I thought she got rid of the manticore." As we reached the third floor, I halted at the entrance to the Magical Creatures Division. Furred books lay scattered all over the carpeted floor, as though they'd crawled off the shelves of their own accord. Some of them were shuffling across the floor, making distressed snapping noises, while others hid in the corners.

"Honestly," said Aunt Adelaide. "Would you go ahead and make sure that book is where it's supposed to be? I'll catch up to you."

Did the book do this? The last thing I wanted was to confront it alone, but it wasn't like I didn't have magic of my own. Pulling out my Biblio-Witch Inventory, I made my way around the corner, following the path I'd walked along yesterday. To my relief, the room from last night remained in the same place as before. Drawing in a deep breath, I tapped the word *open*.

The door sprang open, revealing the small room. The book lay on the table where I'd left it, silent and unmoving. I stopped about a metre away and scanned the cover. I couldn't be sure the text was exactly the same as the journal's, but the book did seem like the type collectors of rare artefacts would do anything to get their hands on. On the other hand, if the murderer had kept tabs on Mr Spencer, they'd know he'd returned the book to the library. Right?

"You again," the book said, its tone dripping with disdain.

I approached the desk. "Yes, it's me."

"Come to give me to another person, have you?" he

said. "For people who claim to care about books, you have no concept of loyalty."

"The person who last took you out of the library is dead," I informed the book. "Someone murdered him this morning, and I think you were the reason."

I'd hoped to shock the book into playing nice. Instead, it screamed. "Murderer! Murderer!"

"Quiet!" I said. "Stop that. We're not sure who killed him, but if you can tell me—"

The book's yells drowned out my voice, and I grabbed for my notebook and pen. I'd never tried a silencing spell before, but for a biblio-witch, any word could become magical.

I pressed the pen to the page and wrote the word *silence!*

Tingles ran from my hand to the page, but the book kept screaming.

I tried again. No result. The third time, I dug the pen so hard into the page that it ripped a hole in the paper, and the book's yells didn't cease.

"You're not powerful enough to subdue the likes of me!" the book crowed.

"Who was the man who took you out of the library?" I bellowed back. "Was there a reason someone might have wanted him dead?"

"No need to shout, my little biblio-witch," said the book.

I glared. My throat hurt, but I'd successfully broken through its screaming. I was beginning to understand why all the books in the Magical Creatures Division had tried to escape their shelves overnight. "Mr Spencer called me and mentioned you a minute before he died. If you know anything, tell me, or else the police will get involved."

"I'd like to see them try," said the book. "I won't talk to you, witchling."

Great. I'd offer compensation, but what could I possibly use to bribe a book? While it seemed sentient, it didn't have Sylvester's ability to change forms or affect the world around it. For all its screaming, the room looked exactly as it had the night before.

"This room's a bit drab, isn't it?" I tried. "If you like, I can ask my aunts to help redecorate the place. Paint the walls, maybe bring you a friend or two…"

"Friends!" The book gave a derisive snort. "Friends. The other books are pathetic and shallow in comparison to my supreme intelligence."

That sounded familiar. "You might get on with Sylvester."

Then again, the idea of the book and the owl teaming up wasn't particularly appealing, either.

The book shuffled its pages together. "Pick me up again, I dare you."

"No thanks. Have you ever met a vampire?"

What was that for, Rory? Sure, Mortimer Vale and his fellow vampire collective were known to be hunters of rare artefacts, but there was nothing connecting them to Mr Spencer's death. As far as I knew, all the guests at the hotel had been human, Mr Spencer included. The vampires weren't the only people who coveted rare books, besides.

The book screamed again. "Evil bloodsuckers! Burn them all! Burn them!"

"All right, all right!" I stepped back as the noise

bounced off the walls, amplified by the narrow space. "I meant—"

The book's yells drowned out my words, making my head pound. *There must be something I can do to stop it from screaming.*

I reached into my bag, my fingers skimming my dad's journal. Then I pulled it out and flipped it open, looking from its text to the symbols on the book's cover. Now I saw both alongside one another, it was clear that it wasn't an exact match after all.

The book ceased mid-scream. "What are you doing?"

I put the journal away. "What's your title? I can't read it."

"None of your business."

"Can you at least show me what language it is? Or let me look inside you without biting me?"

"Fine." The book flipped inside-out and showed me a set of blank pages.

"Hilarious," I said. "I doubt anyone would want to go to the trouble of handling you if you didn't contain any useful information. I'm ordering you to show me, or I'll see if my aunt can't use *her* biblio-witch magic to pry you open."

The book gave another full-volume yell. I pressed my hands to my ears, backing away. Even outside, the walls and floor vibrated with the noise. *Ow.*

"What is going on in here?" Aunt Adelaide appeared behind me. "Stop that at once!"

She walked into the room, pulled out her Biblio-Witch Inventory and tapped a word. I didn't see which it was, but the screaming died down to a low moaning noise.

"Tell me what you know," she commanded.

The book gave another long, drawn-out moan that ended in a series of unflattering insults.

"We're lucky it's not mobile as well as vocal," I remarked. "Did it scare the books outside the room into jumping off the shelves?"

"I'm starting to suspect so." She gave the book a disgruntled look. "Someone was a little too thorough with the security spells, I think. I'll have to lock the door until it calms down."

"Will it calm down, though?" I said. "I mean, it's a book. It's not like it can tire itself out."

The book was theoretically capable of continuing to scream indefinitely—so how were we supposed to question it at all?

Aunt Adelaide rubbed her temples. "I'll think of something. Did you manage to get anything useful out of it before it started screaming?"

"It started yelling as soon as I told it Mr Spencer died," I said. "Then it calmed down when I started suggesting decorating the room... I was trying to think of how to bribe it into giving us answers."

"All right," she said. "We'll go downstairs and talk about our options."

Aunt Adelaide re-locked the door, and we made for the stairs down to the ground floor. On the way, we passed Aunt Candace coming towards us.

"No luck?" she asked. "May I?"

"Feel free," said Aunt Adelaide. "I wouldn't advise touching it, though. It bites."

"Excellent." Aunt Candace hurried along, wearing an expression as though twelve Christmases had arrived at once.

"She might regret that later," I said.

"If there's one thing my sister has alarmingly few of, it's regrets," said Aunt Adelaide.

"I figured." I followed close behind her down the stairs, the part of me relieved not to be dealing with the book warring with the part of me that was certain it must be connected to Mr Spencer's death.

When we were almost at the ground floor, Aunt Adelaide spoke. "You know something, Rory."

There was no accusation in her tone, nor a question. I drew in a breath. "The book… I don't know if you got a good look at the cover, but the text kind of reminded me of the code in my dad's journal at first. I asked the book if it had ever seen a vampire, and that's what set it off screaming again. My biblio-witch magic wasn't strong enough to stop it."

"It's certainly a tricky one," she said. "Let's have a look at that journal again when we're downstairs."

When we reached the ground floor, I pulled out my dad's journal again, skimming through the pages to find a sample of text to compare to the cover. Close up, it wasn't exactly the same, but similar. I'd thought Dad had made up the code himself. Then again, I'd also thought he was normal, non-magical, up until three years after he'd died. Either way, no way to translate the journal had been found, either in our house or in the bookshop where he'd worked.

Aunt Adelaide shook her head. "No, it won't be the same. The text on the cover of the book will be on record, I don't doubt. I *wish* Candace would keep better track of these things. She keeps borrowing our translator spells to assist her in making up her own languages."

"Sounds like her," I said. "When I tried to look inside, the book showed me blank pages. That can't be right, can it?"

"There'd be little value in the book if it was unreadable," she said. "The person who locked it added a large number of security spells. It might not have been one of us, either. Our mother purchased books from all over the world when she opened the library."

Great. For my sanity's sake, I was probably better off leaving it up to Aunt Candace. "Do you need me to do anything else?"

"Can you send Estelle my way?" she asked. "She knows the archives best. We aren't likely to have many visitors today, so handling the desk won't be a huge bother."

"Sure." I made my way across the ground floor, trying unsuccessfully to put the screaming book out of mind.

As for Mr Spencer? The Reaper alone had witnessed his last words, but he'd told me everything he'd heard and there was no sense dragging him into this. His job was to help lost souls, not solve murders—and definitely not get involved with the living. Me included.

"The archives?" said Estelle, looking up when I reached the front desk. "Sure, I'll help out. I don't think anyone's coming in here today. They're too busy nursing hangovers."

Or being questioned by the police. "I don't mind taking over the desk anyway." I'd be more useful here than trying to squeeze answers out of that screaming book.

On the desk, the logbook lay open on a date almost a year ago. Estelle must have been looking through it to find when Mr Spencer had borrowed the book, and by the looks of things, she hadn't found it yet. I hadn't progressed to covering long-term loans in my biblio-witch training yet, so the logbook made little sense to me. I turned the page over, starting to understand why my aunts couldn't recall loaning out the book. The number of clients they'd handled in the last year must be in the thousands, if not more.

A clicking noise drew my attention to the door, which drifted closed as though prompted by a faint breeze. The small hairs rose on the back of my neck at the sight of a beautiful woman standing in front of the desk.

"Oh, am I interrupting something?" said Evangeline, the leader of the vampires.

5

The vampires' leader smiled. As usual, her appearance was impeccable, her dark hair glossy and styled, her lips painted blood red and parted just enough to show her pointed canines.

I kept my gaze on the desk, forcing my mind to focus on that without letting any thoughts sneak through for her to leap on and use against me. "Is there something you'd like?"

"A book," she said. "Why else would I visit the library?"

To get your hands on my dad's journal. Which we both know, but I won't mention it before you do.

"You heard he died," I said. "Mr Spencer. Right?"

"Yes, I did," she said. "But I'm not here to fish for gossip. I already know what I need to."

Hmm. "Then why are you here?"

"I was interested in the book the hotel guest had in his possession. I heard he returned it to the library, so I'd like to check out the title now it's available."

That wasn't a confession, surely. Not that I could make an open challenge against her, considering her authority.

"The book," I said, "is not taking the loss of Mr Spencer well. It's throwing a tantrum, actually. So it's… not available. Not to anyone."

Her brow arched. "Oh? That's a shame."

"Do you know who Mr Spencer was? The man who had the book?"

"I'm afraid I've never met him in my life. I merely heard the book was returned, not who last checked it out."

"You heard… you read someone's mind, didn't you?" I said. "You haven't seen any of us since before he died. Who else knew what book he had?"

Mr Blake, perhaps, which meant she'd been snooping around the hotel.

"There's no reason to act so suspicious, Aurora. I heard the thoughts of some of the hotel guests after the police let them go. I was looking for something quite different at the time, but if it's too soon to ask, I can come back later."

"My aunt is working out how to handle the book," I said. "It's likely to be at least a day, if not more."

Okay, perhaps I was being unfair. It might be simple curiosity that had driven her to come here, not a guilty conscience. Not that I was certain Evangeline *had* a conscience. Some vampires, like my Aunt Candace's ex, Dominic, acted more or less human, but people like her seemed to get a kick out of scaring the living hell out of people. The mind-reading advantage alone was reason enough to be wary of her.

"I will come back tomorrow, then," she said. "Such a strange murder case. A tragic one, really."

The day Evangeline felt concern for a human would be the day Aunt Candace retired from publishing books.

There came a shrieking noise from somewhere above our heads. Speaking of Aunt Candace, I'd bet she'd done something to tick off the book even more. The leader of the vampires raised an eyebrow as the screaming rose in volume.

"Is someone having difficulties?" she asked.

"That's the book," I said. "My aunts are trying to subdue it, but it's dangerous to let it out of the library until it's calmed down. And even then, I'm not sure it'll let you read it."

"Let me?" She arched a brow. "I doubt a simple book will be that much trouble for *me*."

I had to admit, part of me would be all too happy to foist the screaming book on her so we'd have it off our hands. But whatever her reasons for wanting the book, I'd bet they had nothing to do with solving the mystery of Mr Spencer's death.

"I'll see you later, Aurora."

And in a blink, Evangeline was gone.

I released a breath, the tension I hadn't been entirely aware of seeping out of my body. Perhaps she didn't have ulterior motives, but I'd eat my notebook before I admitted she wasn't interested in whether or not the book had caused Mr Spencer's death. The last time we'd spoken, she'd tried to bribe me into handing over my dad's journal, and while I now knew the code inside it didn't match the book upstairs, Dominic's last message to me before his death had warned me not to trust her.

The screaming grew even louder, and my pounding headache came back with a vengeance. Covering my ears,

I headed into the archives and found Aunt Adelaide and Estelle surrounded by stacks of old logbooks. "What *is* she doing to that book?"

"If I had to guess?" said Aunt Adelaide. "Candace decided to probe the book for information. Would you mind having a look up there?"

"I'll deal with it this time." Estelle bounded to her feet.

"There's no need," said Aunt Candace's raised voice from the stairs. "We're coming down."

"No, we're not," yelled the book. "I won't have this! I won't!"

Oh, no.

"What're you bringing it down here for?" said Aunt Adelaide in irate tones.

"Because it's a fascinating piece of work as well as potential evidence in a murder case," said Aunt Candace, raising her voice even louder over the book's screaming.

"It's also screaming bloody murder," said Aunt Adelaide. "And it'll scare off our patrons."

Estelle walked down the row of shelves. "I'll get her to put it in an empty room with a silencing spell on it before anyone else comes in."

"Good plan." I went with her to accost Aunt Candace, who descended the staircase with the book held in a firm grip. She wore thick gloves up to her elbows, which was probably the only reason she still had all her fingers.

"I'm not taking it back upstairs," she said. "That's twice it's wrecked the Magical Creatures Division. Half the books jumped off their shelves when it started squawking."

"Cass is going to be thrilled, if she's up there." Estelle beckoned her aunt to follow her towards the back of the ground floor. "Quick, get it into an empty room before anyone else comes in and hears it."

"Oh, don't be ridiculous," said Aunt Candace, stepping off the stairs. The book rustled its pages, but she held them clamped shut as she carried the book through into an empty classroom at the back of the ground floor.

"I *suppose* this will do." She held the book at arm's length as it tried to snap at her. "Don't you look at me like that, you're lucky I haven't recycled you."

Estelle pulled out her Biblio-Witch Inventory and tapped a word. At once, the door closed on Aunt Candace and the noise quietened. "That'll hold it for a while. If she expects to get answers when it's wailing like that, she'll be disappointed."

"That seems to be its default state." There must be another way to find out what information the book contained. The obvious source of knowledge on the library's contents was the Forbidden Room, but I hadn't seen Sylvester since that morning, and it wouldn't surprise me if he took the rest of the day off in protest at the noise.

"I'd lock the door, but Aunt Candace would just unlock it again." Estelle tutted. "I'm impressed you lasted more than a minute in the same room as that thing."

"Me too, believe me." Rubbing my temples, I walked with Estelle back to the front desk. The library was just closing for lunch, so I volunteered to buy something from Zee's bakery while Estelle and Aunt Adelaide resumed searching the archives. Getting out into the fresh air improved my mood considerably, and I returned from the bakery to find Sylvester sitting on the front desk.

"There you are." I put down the bag of sandwiches. "I need to ask a question."

"You're not supposed to ask me directly," the owl said. "You know where the Book of Questions is. If you insist on asking me a question, use the book."

"Why?" I said. "It'd save time if you just told me."

"You—" He broke off as a furious scream echoed from the back of the ground floor. Oh, no. Estelle's spell had run out already?

"What is that ghastly noise?" Sylvester launched into flight, trying unsuccessfully to fly with one wing over his ears.

"That's what I wanted to ask the room about," I said. "That book won't talk to any of us or even let us look inside it without throwing a screaming fit."

"What book is that?" He flew through the stacks. Resigned, I abandoned my bag of sandwiches on the front desk and followed him in the direction of the noise.

At the back of the ground floor, the classroom door lay open. Inside, Aunt Candace stood on the desk, using her wand to bounce the book off the floor, over and over again.

"Aunt Candace, everyone in the library can hear that racket," I said to her.

She didn't turn around. "I'll break you, book, and find your secrets. You'll see if I don't."

Sylvester swooped into the room and flew above the bouncing book. "You're an ugly little specimen, aren't you?"

The book stopped screaming for an instant. "What are you?"

"That's a highly personal question." The owl flew in

another circle, its claws narrowly missing the bouncing book. "You're just a sentience spell, aren't you?"

"Yes, it is," said Aunt Candace. "One with a right pair of lungs on it, metaphorically speaking."

"What language is on the cover?" I asked Sylvester, but the book's indignant shouts drowned out my words. The owl's hooting added to the overall noise, making it impossible to make myself heard. Of course letting Sylvester near the book was a disaster waiting to happen.

"Rory, I think we should leave Aunt Candace and Sylvester to it," Estelle said in my ear. "Also, there's someone at the front desk."

"I give it two minutes before they run away." Shaking my head, I left the classroom behind and walked to the front desk.

Beside the door, Blair and Nathan stood with their ears covered and their faces screwed up against the racket coming from the back.

"Is this a bad time?" asked Blair.

"Don't worry," I said, in a failed attempt at nonchalance. "We're dealing with a book."

Screaming rang through the lobby, accompanied by full-volume hooting from the owl.

"Do the books normally scream like that?" Blair asked.

"Sometimes." It sounded like Sylvester had decided to turn it into a competition as to who could make the loudest noise.

"MIAOW." The fluffy black cat from earlier sat at Blair's feet, a disgruntled expression on his face.

"Maybe we should have left him at home." Blair took a step forward, her eyes widening at the sight of the towering shelves. "Wow. This place really is as big as it looks on the outside."

Her unfeigned awe sounded familiar. *Did she grow up in the normal world, like me?* Okay, the library was jaw-dropping even by the standards of the magical world, but there was something about her unrestrained shock and delight at the sight of the library which reminded me of my first time here.

"I can show you around later," I said. "After the book's calmed down. Want me to show you around town, since you're new here?"

It'd be a good opportunity to speak to Blair about Mr Spencer, if nothing else, and anything that got us away from the screaming book was a bonus.

Blair dragged her gaze from the bookshelves. "Okay, give me the tour."

"I'll handle Sylvester," Estelle said from behind me.

"Thanks so much." I snagged a sandwich from the bag on the desk and led the way out of the library. "When did you two arrive, then?"

"Yesterday morning," said Nathan. "We didn't do much except check into the hotel, and most places were closed. Same today."

"Some places are open." I led them through the town square, pointing out the highlights like Zee's bakery and the familiar shop. Blair eyed everything in an awestruck manner that made me suspect this was her first time visiting a town like ours, though she must live in a magical community to know of our existence.

"We've already seen the main part of town, but it's much quieter today," Nathan commented as we passed the clock tower on the way to the seafront.

"Yeah, the whole town comes out to celebrate the new year," I said. "I only moved here just over a month ago, so I'm fairly new to this, too."

"You did?" said Blair. "So… you're from another magical town."

I turned to Blair. "You're a normal. I mean, from the normal world. Aren't you?"

"Am I that obvious?" She smiled. "I'm a witch, but I grew up in a family of normals."

"I did, too," I said. "My dad married a normal and moved away from the library before I was born, so I didn't find out it existed until my aunts got in touch after he passed away. How about you?"

"I was adopted," said Blair. "My foster parents had no idea about the magical world. I didn't either until I wandered into it by accident. Have you heard of Fairy Falls?"

"No, but I've only lived here for a couple of months," I said. "I don't know about any of the other magical cities and towns. What made you decide to come here on holiday? The library?"

"One of the reasons," said Nathan. "We both wanted to pick somewhere on the coast, despite the weather."

"Always a gamble this time of year," I said. "So you're… a wizard?"

That didn't seem right. I couldn't put my finger on it, but the label didn't quite fit Nathan. He seemed comfortable enough here that he didn't strike me as a normal, either, but I didn't pick up on any paranormal vibes from him.

"No, I'm a security guard," he said. "Blair and I wanted

to come to the library earlier, but we got held up at the hotel."

Now's my cue.

"Edwin didn't give you too much of a hard time?" I said. "He's the police chief. Generally a nice guy, but I doubt he wanted to start the year with a tragic death." Or a screaming book, for that matter.

"Oh, the elf policeman," said Blair. "No, he just asked us all a few questions. Those trolls he works with looked mean, but they weren't as rough as the police in Fairy Falls."

"Who runs the police there?" I asked.

"Gargoyles," said Nathan. "They're not friendly."

"I've never met one," I admitted. "Edwin questioned all the guests? Were there any he seemed to suspect more than others?"

"You mean Mr Blake?" said Blair. "The guy who argued with Mr Spencer before he died? His interview was longer than the rest of ours, but I don't know what they asked him. There was also old Mr Dreyer, the man who said he was a collector. He looked super uncomfortable after they interviewed him."

The collector guy. Hmm.

"Why are you asking?" she said. "Curiosity?"

"Pretty much." I weighed the odds. She and Nathan didn't strike me as likely to be involved with whatever Mr Spencer had been mixed up in, and Blair's skill might be an asset if we were to get answers out of the book. She might even be able to learn more from the guests without causing suspicion, which was always a bonus. "The book Mr Spencer returned to the library is the one we're having trouble with. It's the type of book targeted by collectors and thieves, so there's a small chance it might be connected to his death, since he was the last person to hold it. Don't tell anyone I said that, though."

"Really?" Interest stirred in her expression. "Why, is it dangerous?"

Only to the eardrums of anyone who gets too close. "Possibly. Mr Spencer called the library right before he died, trying to tell me something about the book. That's why I was at the hotel."

Blair's eyes rounded. "Really?"

"Can you tell if *anyone* is lying?" I asked. "No exceptions?"

She blinked. "Yeah. Anyone living, anyway."

Hmm. Would a sentient book count as 'living'? One way to find out.

6

Luck was with us. A blissful silence greeted us upon our return to the library, where once again, Blair stopped to admire the storeys of towering shelves, layered like a wedding cake. I grinned. I'd worn the same expression when I'd first encountered the library, too.

"Miaow," said Sky. He looked unimpressed, but then again, he was a cat.

"I have to head outside and make a phone call," said Nathan. "You can find what you're looking for, right, Blair?"

"Sure." She waved him off. "He gets a lot of people hassling him, even when he's supposed to be on holiday. Anyway, I want to see more of this place."

"Is your cat okay with birds?" I asked.

"Uh, it depends," she said. "Why?"

"My familiar is a crow," I explained. "I thought you might like to meet him."

"Ooh, I've never met a crow familiar before," said Blair. "Sky is generally fine with other witches' familiars. He tends to ignore them, even other cats."

"Okay." I snapped my fingers. "Jet, we need you."

The little crow flew down to land on my shoulder.

"Hello, partner," said Jet.

Blair jumped. "He talks?"

"I used a communicating spell that got a bit out of hand," I explained. "I thought only my family could understand him."

"Huh." She frowned. "Well, I heard him loud and clear."

Weird. The spell I'd used wasn't supposed to be applied long-term, so perhaps it came with side effects. Jet had been hurt when I'd suggested removing the spell, though, and I liked having a familiar I could really talk to. One who wasn't Sylvester.

Sky gave a brief look at my familiar, then looked away, indifferent, as Jet continued to perch on my shoulder.

"I'll give you the tour, anyway," I said. "Does Sky want to come with us, or would he rather do his own thing?"

"Miaow," said Sky. I didn't need to be able to speak cat to understand he meant, *I'll do as I wish.*

"All right, then." I circled the desk. "The archives are back here, and over there is the Reading Corner."

I took Blair around the highlights of the ground floor, pointing out the main areas of interest. Blair's awed expression hadn't faded in the slightest by the time we reached the front desk again.

"You said you wanted to see something in particular?" I asked. "Fair warning, it'd take you all day to show you every corner of the place, so if there's one section you really want to see, I should take you there first."

Blair hesitated. "Uh… I'm looking for anything you have on fairies."

"Fairies," I repeated. "That's a new one for me, but if it's magical, we've got it covered."

I picked up the paper on the front desk which listed all the library's main sections and ran a fingertip down the list. I knew most of the basics, but fairies wouldn't be located within the same area as magical creatures. They'd be more likely to be in the 'magical beings' division, I imagined. "Third floor. Lead the way, Jet."

The little crow flew ahead towards the stairs, while Blair followed with her head tilted back to admire the curving balconies and staircases.

"Watch out for the missing steps," I told her. "It's probably better to keep your eyes on your feet while you're climbing. Sometimes the stairs move."

"Oh, neat," said Blair. "They're just like the staircases at Hogwarts, then?"

"Kind of," I said. "Some more than others. In the Dimensional Studies section, everything moves, including the shelves."

"Awesome."

"Not when you're trying to put a book back into place." I climbed ahead of her, one eye on the steps beneath my feet. "We need to climb all the way up to the third floor. No detours, or else we'll be here all week."

"And I thought the campus library was confusing," Blair remarked. "How do you remember the way? Is there a map?"

"Not exactly." I reached the first floor and continued to the next set of stairs. "Time and space can get a little hazy here. There are places that move around, and there's the invisible corridor…"

"Can you show me that one?" she said. "I mean… not show me. You know what I mean."

"I would if I could, but nobody knows where it is," I admitted. "My grandma's the person who created the place, and she died without leaving a map, so we have to make do with what we have."

"Then every day must be a new adventure, right?"

"You bet." Okay, maybe I was showing off a little, but how many chances would I get to give someone from the normal world a tour of the library? Even most witches and wizards from outside the town didn't react with the same level of awe as Blair did.

We reached the Magical Beings Division after only two wrong turnings, neither of which involved falling through the floor or running into another talkative book. To my relief, the door marked FAIRIES stood near the front, without any of the obvious warning signs.

I pushed the door open and found what appeared to be a cross between a forest and an underground cave. The oak bookshelves curved along with the walls as though they'd grown out of the cave itself, while roots spread beneath our feet and vines and plants sprouted between the shelves. *This is pretty cool.*

Jet amused himself flying around the forested cave while the two of us checked out the books on the shelves, most of which were written in languages that presumably belonged to the fairies. I'd spent so long immersed in the witches' world that I often forgot there were countless paranormals who didn't live in the same places as humans did.

"Found what you were looking for?" I asked Blair, after about ten minutes of browsing the shelves. "I don't know about you, but I'm not fluent in fairy languages."

She shook her head. "No. It was kind of a long shot, but thanks anyway. Fairies are stingy about sharing information with humans."

"Want to head back downstairs?" I asked. "I can show you a few more highlights on the way."

I decided to skip over the vampire in the basement, having had about enough of vampires for one day, but almost everything I showed her received the same awed reaction.

"I can't believe you get to work here," she said, when we returned to the front desk. "I think I'd never leave."

"I'm often tempted not to," I admitted. "What do you do for a living, then?"

"I work for a paranormal recruitment firm at home in Fairy Falls," she said. "We help employers find the perfect employees."

"Oh, you mean like graduate job recruitment, except…"

"For paranormals," she finished. "So we handle grumpy wizards who can't keep an apprentice, and people looking for specialised staff like unicorn handlers."

"Unicorns?" I said. "I haven't seen one of those yet. Though I wouldn't mention it in front of my cousin, Cass. She has a habit of finding rare magical animals and bringing them into the library when my aunts aren't looking. If you saw someone wading into the sea last night, that was her."

"Ah," said Blair. "Yeah, there's never a dull moment in the magical world. I only have a few days off from work over the holidays, but Nathan and I decided to get out of town for a bit. I'm glad we did."

"Is there anything else you wanted to look for, aside from fairies?" I asked.

"Um…" She paused. "This is going to sound weird, but do you have a section in here on magical codes, and how to translate them? Not like the fairy language, but something a bit more specialist."

The image of the journal flashed before my eyes. I hadn't mentioned it aloud. She couldn't know about it, right? "I think that would be Aunt Adelaide's area."

"All right," she said. "It's okay if not. Basically, a fairy left a note for me written in code, and I can't read it. But I trust the person who left it for me, so it must be translatable."

I might not be able to sense lies the way she could, but her tone rang with sincerity. "Okay, I'll ask my aunt."

Someone cleared their throat nearby. I turned around, unsurprised to see Aunt Candace lurking behind a shelf, pen and notebook in hand.

"That," I said, "is my other aunt, Candace. She writes novels."

"I dabble." Aunt Candace walked into view, her pen and notebook vanishing as she did so. "Did I hear someone mention magical codes?"

"I have a note written in a code I need to translate," said Blair. "I was told a library like yours might be able to help me work it out."

"We don't—" I began, but Aunt Candace interrupted.

"Yes," she said. "We have a spell that can translate hundreds of common codes, including languages that don't exist yet."

"Yet?" echoed Blair. "How does that work?"

"I'm lost, too," I said, equally bewildered. "What spell is this? Why did nobody tell me about it before?"

Aunt Candace tutted. "That'll be my sister being secretive again, I don't doubt. I'm sure she won't mind me borrowing it."

She pulled out her Biblio-Witch Inventory and tapped a word. At once, a large hardback book appeared in her hand in a flash of light. At least, I thought it was a book, until she pulled the cover back to reveal the inside of a box. "Not bad spellwork."

"What *is* that?" I asked.

"There's no need to sound so accusing," said Aunt Candace, holding out her free hand. "Put the letter in here and the spell will work its magic."

Blair pulled a roll of paper from her pocket and hesitantly handed it over to Aunt Candace. With an eager expression on her face, she dropped the paper into the box. When the lid closed, the whole book—I mean, box—glowed bright green.

"Is it supposed to do that?" I asked.

Instead of answering, Aunt Candace laid the box on the desk. "Leave it for twenty minutes or so. I'll call you here when it's done."

I studied the box. A label on the cover said, *Prototype. Do not touch. That means you, Candace.* "Did Aunt Adelaide give you permission to borrow that?"

"What do you think?" She shook her head. "She's been sitting on this for weeks. It's about time we put it to use."

I hope she's tested it first. I could think of only one reason Aunt Adelaide would work on a top-secret spell which translated magical codes… to translate my dad's journal.

Aunt Candace shooed Blair and me away. "Go and entertain yourselves elsewhere, the two of you."

Giving my aunt a look telling her we'd be having words later, I walked with Blair towards the back of the ground floor. "I hope it works, but you might want to run for the hills when my Aunt Adelaide comes back and finds out her sister borrowed her spell."

Blair winced. "I hope it doesn't damage the paper. I only have one copy."

"Nah, it wasn't Aunt Candace who made the spell. If it was, I'd worry." I halted in the Reading Corner. "I actually needed your help with something, if that's okay."

"Me?" Her brow furrowed. "Help with what?"

"I need you to help me question a book, using your lie-sensing ability," I said. "That is… if it works on sentient books, anyway. We've tried everything else, and I'm not sure we have any kind of lie-detecting spell that works as well as your talent does."

"Sentient?" Her eyes flared with interest. "I've never seen a sentient book before. But I guess you deal with that kind of thing all the time here."

"It's actually a new one for me," I said. "The book Mr Spencer returned to the library before his death is under a sentience spell. There's a chance it knows why he was killed, but it keeps throwing tantrums whenever any of us try to get answers from it. That was the book you heard screaming earlier. It might be that we're wasting our time trying to question it, but I wondered if you might want to give it a try."

"Sure. No problem." Blair must know I hadn't told her everything, if her lie-detecting ability could sense such things, but I'd piqued her curiosity. As far as I knew, she didn't know anything about the vampires or anyone who'd have reason to target our books, so there was no danger of her telling tales.

Blair and I approached the classroom behind the Reading Corner. Aunt Candace had left the door locked, so I pulled out my Biblio-Witch Inventory.

"What's that?" asked Blair.

I ran my fingertip down the page. "This is my family's magical talent."

I tapped the word *open,* and the door unlocked itself. I braced myself to hear screaming, but the book was silent. *Okay. Good start.* Just as long as Sylvester stayed away.

"Jet, can you wait outside?" I whispered to the crow.

"Certainly, partner!" My familiar flew down to land on a nearby shelf, shedding leaves from the fairy cave in the process. Meanwhile, Blair and I entered the room. *Here goes nothing.*

"You're new," said the book.

"It can see me?" Blair jumped a little. "How?"

"How do you think?" said the book. "I'm all-seeing."

At least it wasn't screaming this time. I moved closer to the table. "Would someone have a reason to commit murder to get their hands on you?"

"Yes. People will commit murder over anything."

That's not much of an answer.

"What do you contain information about?" I asked. "Dark magic?"

"Dark magic!" The book's cover seemed to meld itself

to the pages as Blair reached out a hesitant hand. "Don't you touch me, witchling. I've had enough of being poked and prodded around."

"We'll leave you alone if you tell me if you know who murdered Mr Spencer."

There was a long pause. "Do you expect me to know everything about every human who touches me?"

"That wasn't an answer," Blair said.

"What's it to you?" said the book. "Murder indeed. Do you accuse all your books of inspiring deadly deeds?"

"No, but Mr Spencer called me on the phone and was in the middle of mentioning something about you when he died," I said. "What was he saying?"

"I can't read minds, idiot," said the book.

"Oi," said Blair. "That's not very nice of you. How do we open you, then?"

The book snapped its pages like teeth, and she withdrew her fingers out the way. "You don't."

There must be a way. Mr Spencer must have known— not to mention at least one of my aunts.

"The book's telling the truth," Blair murmured. "Maybe it only opens for certain people."

"Don't *you* sound sure of yourself," he said. "What're you, then? Another witch, yes, but not just that."

"Yes, I am." Blair leaned in. "What are you, then?"

"A book."

"Guess I walked into that one," said Blair. "What information do you contain?"

"Nothing that would interest you."

She frowned. "True. Huh."

"You can sense truth from lies?" said the book. "I'm not playing this game. I quit."

"Don't be difficult." I gave the book a stern look. "Why wouldn't your information interest us? Answer me."

"Would you like me to start screaming again?" said the book.

"Not really." I sighed. "I think we'd better try again later."

We left the room. At least I'd got a clue… of sorts. If Mr Spencer had a trick for opening the book and shutting it up, though, it was beyond me.

Sylvester sat on the bookshelf outside, tilting his head when Blair and I walked past.

"Hello," said Sylvester. "New in town, are you?"

"Oh, he talks too?" said Blair.

"He does," I said. "That's Sylvester. He works for the library."

"The library works for me," he corrected, ruffling his feathers. "Poking that book again, were you? I've never seen a sentience charm so sharply crafted before."

"Is that what it is?" I asked. "Can you undo the spell?"

"Me? I'm just an owl."

"You know what I mean."

"MIAOW." Sky looked up at the owl with the most disapproving expression I'd ever seen on a cat's face. Did the cat somehow sense that he wasn't a real owl? He hadn't had an issue with Jet at all.

"Miaow yourself," said Sylvester. "We don't allow cats in here."

"There's no rule against them," I said, for Blair's benefit. "Sylvester dislikes sharing his space."

"We're leaving," Blair said hastily. "We're just waiting for Rory's aunt to finish translating something for me."

"Stole Adelaide's spell, did she?" Sylvester hooted with laughter. "This, I'd like to see."

"Even *you* knew about it?" I shook my head at him.

"There's nothing I don't know," the owl called after us as we walked back to the front desk.

"Here it is," said Aunt Candace, waving her wand over the translator spell. "Ta da."

The box sprang open. Blair reached into it and pulled out two pieces of paper. One was the original note, and the other was written in English. I caught the word *fairy* and averted my gaze. The paper must be important to Blair, but I wouldn't pry into its contents, not when I had enough secrets of my own.

Blair clutched the paper and slipped it into her pocket. "Thanks. I'll read it later."

"You're welcome," said Aunt Candace. "Enjoy your stay. And please keep your cat to yourself."

I looked down at Sky, who now sat on the desk, glaring at Sylvester.

"Sky," said Blair, beckoning to her familiar. "C'mon. we're leaving."

The cat hissed, then hopped off the desk and followed her to the door.

"Would it be possible for you to talk to the other guests at the hotel if you see them?" I asked Blair. "Perhaps one of them knows how to open the book. Mr Blake might, since he and Mr Spencer knew one another."

"I can try," she said. "Mr Dreyer knows about old books, so he might know."

"Mr Dreyer, the relic collector?" I said. "Not sure the book counts as a relic, but the two of them were talking the night before he died."

Her eyes widened in understanding. "Sure. I can have a word with him. I'll drop by tomorrow and let you know if I find anything out."

"Cheers." I waved goodbye to her. I'd considered asking Mr Blake if his friend had been able to read the book, but maybe I was better off letting Blair do the questioning. She seemed to have more experience than I did, with good reason, considering her lie-sensing power. And she wouldn't have to be direct with her questioning, for the same reason. Any lie, however minor, might point her to the culprit.

Aunt Candace clucked her teeth behind me. "That's one interesting friend you've made."

I wheeled on the spot. The translator spell had vanished, as though it'd never existed. "Is Aunt Adelaide going to notice you borrowed her spell?"

"Oh, don't get your knickers in a twist, Rory. I know for a fact she planned to use it on that blasted book as soon as it stopped screaming long enough."

I folded my arms. "Good, because you probably just ruined her big reveal."

"Big reveal? More like she forgot about it," she said. "What with you people running around solving murders. Don't think I didn't hear you talking to that Blair."

"She's staying at the hotel. It's hard *not* to get involved." I shook my head. "We still need to work out who Mr Spencer was, why he died, and why he called me moments before his death."

She clucked her teeth. "Pity we can't get the dead to speak to us, isn't it?"

That's one way of putting it. Even the Reaper couldn't,

though it was starting to look like he'd need to stay involved in this case one way or another.

But was it possible to involve Xavier in my life without getting my heart tangled up in the process?

7

When I went downstairs the following morning, I found Estelle and Aunt Adelaide sitting at the kitchen table with the translator spell of all things. I stood there in the doorway, my mouth hanging open.

"There's more toast over there," said Aunt Adelaide. "And yes, I know Candace borrowed my spell yesterday. She and I had a little chat this morning."

I glanced at the box. "Sorry. I should have stopped her."

"There's no stopping my sister when she's on a mission," said Aunt Adelaide. "Besides, I gathered the young woman's request was important."

"Yeah, but I'm glad it worked," I said. "She didn't even test it first."

"Luckily, *I* did." Aunt Adelaide gave the box a shake. "It doesn't seem to be cooperating with me today. This is why I wanted to do some more testing before putting it to work."

"On my dad's journal?"

She gave me a brief glance, then the box spat a few green sparks into the air. She waved her wand, coughing. "As you can see, it needs some more fine-tuning."

I held my breath against the burning smell and moved the coffee pot out of reach before a spark fell into it.

"We've found out more about this Mr Spencer, though," said Estelle. "Seems he's travelled all over. Lived in dozens of locations."

"All magical?" I sat down at the table, pouring myself some coffee from the pot.

"No," she said. "That's the odd part. I haven't managed to nail down where he was born, but he's lived in cities like London at least as often as he's lived in magical towns like ours. It seems he didn't like to settle in any one place for long."

"For the last few years, at least," added Aunt Adelaide. "According to Edwin, he had no family within reach, so his body is being held in storage until they know if he has anyone to contact."

I loaded my plate and dug in. "Did you figure out when he checked out the book?"

"Not yet," said Estelle. "We don't think he stayed in town either, though we'll be checking with Frederick. The odds of him picking a different hotel are low, considering Frederick's is the most popular. If his details are somewhere in the hotel records, it'll give us a clue about which dates in the logbook to check."

I chewed a mouthful of toast. "So he came to town for the sole purpose of borrowing that book?"

"Perhaps," said Aunt Adelaide, rising to her feet and levitating her plate over to the sink. "His friend Mr Blake seems to have a similar history, though as far as I know, it's his first time visiting Ivory Beach. That's as much as I managed to get from Edwin, anyway."

"You mean that Mr Blake guy also travelled the world and never settled in one place?" I asked. "What did the two of them even do for a living?"

"*That*, I don't know." Her brow furrowed. "It seems odd, but perhaps they have the same interests and that's what drew them together. In any case, it's hard to draw any conclusions until we get more in-depth information from Edwin."

Perhaps Blair had had better luck questioning Mr Blake, but I'd have to wait until the library opened to speak to her.

I was finishing up my coffee when Aunt Candace bounded into the room. "I found it."

"Found what?" I put my mug down.

"That." She threw a sheet of paper onto the table. "I've worked out what the title of the book is."

"You didn't even know what the *title* was?" I said disbelievingly.

"Why are you so surprised?" said Aunt Candace. "There's a whole section of title-less volumes, not to mention the ones with invisible text."

"Aunt Candace, stop teasing her," said Estelle sternly. "You're right to be concerned, Rory. The book had a placeholder title in our records, but it'll be easier to track it down if we have the translated version. How did you figure it out, Aunt Candace?"

"I put it in the translator box," she said proudly. "It nearly exploded in the process, but I managed to salvage it."

"You put it *inside* the translator box without knowing if it would work?" Aunt Adelaide's face went brick red. "Is that why it's spitting sparks at people? Couldn't you have waited for me to finish the box before you gave it a test run?"

"You're the most ungrateful bunch of individuals I've ever met." Aunt Candace thrust the paper into her sister's face. "There."

Aunt Adelaide's gaze fixed on the page. "I could have worked that one out without breaking a spell that's taken me weeks to make."

"Aunt Candace said it works on languages that don't exist yet." I gave her a pointed look. "Which makes no sense to me."

"It makes perfect sense," said Aunt Candace. "*That* book, though, can't be fully translated until we get the blasted thing open."

"Convenient," muttered Aunt Adelaide. "A book that hides its contents… I *know* I've dealt with it before, but it must be a very long time since I've handled that particular title."

Aunt Candace gave her a disgruntled look. "I really don't know why I bother with you people. Are there any other mundane chores you need me to do?"

"No, but I should mention Evangeline was here yesterday," I added. "She heard about the book Mr Spencer returned and wanted to express her interest in having a look at it herself."

"She did?" Aunt Adelaide's eyes widened. "Did she give her reasons?"

"Apparently she's interested in any rare and valuable

books," I said. "Same as usual. I told her it was screaming at everyone, and she cleared off."

Aunt Candace grabbed a piece of toast, a calculating expression on her face. "Does *she* want to take it off our hands?"

"No," said Aunt Adelaide, me, and Estelle at the same time.

"Don't you even think about it, Candace." Aunt Adelaide picked up the translator spell. "I'm going to fix this."

"I take it this isn't a good time to try it on my dad's journal?" I turned in my seat to face her in the doorway.

Aunt Adelaide's expression softened. "When it's ready, I'll let you know."

That would have to do for now. "At least my dad's journal has never started screaming or biting anyone."

"You aren't wrong," said Estelle. "Aunt Candace, did you leave the book locked in the classroom overnight?"

"Where else would it be?" She picked up another piece of toast and walked out behind her sister, leaving Estelle and me alone.

"How is it that none of us can open the book?" I asked. "I thought since it's our property, it'd at least work for one of us."

"You'd be surprised," said Estelle. "There are plenty of books we've purchased, or our grandmother has, without instructions as to how to open them. If someone wants to borrow them, there's usually extensive questioning involved, but I assume that one went through without any trouble."

No trouble... except for the fact that the guy who'd borrowed it was dead, and nobody could remember loaning it to him. Not even Sylvester—though he dealt with late fees, not loans, and he claimed most of his knowledge lay inside the Forbidden Room. Let's face it, though— everything *about* that book screamed trouble.

"It's almost opening time." Estelle got to her feet. "I'll be at the front desk."

"Right behind you." I drained the rest of my coffee and followed her into the main part of the library. There, we found Aunt Adelaide beside the front desk, talking to Blair Wilkes.

"Hey," I said. "Back for more?"

The sound of the book yelling came from behind the shelves. "Oh, no," said Aunt Adelaide. "The spell wore off again. You can help Blair, can't you, Rory?"

"Sure." I turned to Blair. "As you might have gathered, we've made zero progress on the screaming book. Anyway, did you have the chance to speak to the other guests at the hotel yesterday?"

"I did," she said. "Mr Dreyer claimed to have never met any of the other guests before, including Mr Spencer. I tried to get him onto the subject of the book by asking why he was in town, but he kept evading my questions. But he did mention something odd."

"Oh?" I lowered my voice when the screaming came to an abrupt stop.

Blair glanced over her shoulder. "He said he was up late last night and heard a weird noise outside. He looked out of his window and saw a figure standing there looking up at the hotel. When he saw him looking, the guy disappeared *fast*. According to Mr Dreyer, it must have been a vampire."

A *vampire.* My heartbeat quickened. "Did he recognise who the vampire was? Or give a description?"

"Not a useful one," said Blair. "He described him as a tall man dressed in dark clothing. He's not from around here, so he wouldn't know any of the local vampires on sight. He wasn't lying, for what it's worth."

That meant he wouldn't know if the vampire was from Ivory Beach or not. Even I hadn't met many of the locals, Evangeline being an obvious exception.

"Your lie-sensing power didn't go off, then?" I asked.

"No, it didn't," she said. "As for Mr Blake, he was out all day. I didn't see him. I think he's avoiding the hotel, though he might have been called back to the police for questioning again."

I hadn't heard about Edwin calling people back in, so I'd assumed he'd concluded Mr Spencer's death was a tragic accident and nothing more. As for Mr Dreyer's claims, I shouldn't jump to conclusions. Vampires wandered around at night, after all. On the other hand, there was little reason one might wander over to the hotel in the middle of the night and stare through the guests' windows. That didn't strike me as a normal thing to do, but was anything the vampires did remotely normal?

"Did Mr Dreyer tell anyone else what he saw?" I asked.

"He mentioned it at breakfast," she said. "But Mr Blake told him he was imagining it, and pretty much ordered him to stop scaring the other guests. I asked if he had a particular reason to be concerned, but he didn't answer. I haven't seen him since."

Had Mr Blake taken off because he had something to hide? Maybe I was reading too much into it, but after what I'd heard about Mr Blake having the same apparent nomadic lifestyle as Mr Spencer, it cemented my certainty that the two had been more than buddies who ran into one another occasionally.

"Do the other guests know about your ability?" Maybe Mr Blake knew, and that's why he'd disappeared—to avoid Blair asking him any questions where he'd have to lie.

"I guess they might have heard Nathan and me talking," she said. "What, you think Mr Blake knew more than he let on? He didn't say where he was going today, but I can talk to him again later if there's anything more you want me to find out."

"Did he come to town alone, then?" I asked.

"He did," she said. "He hasn't told us any personal details about his life. Said he worked as a freelancer, and as far as I know, that's the truth."

"Freelancer covers a lot of things," I said. "Mr Spencer has a similar history. My aunts ran a background check, and it sounds like both of them moved around frequently without settling in one place."

"Both of them did?" she said. "Did they travel together?"

"It doesn't sound like it," I said, "but they did both end up in Ivory Beach at the same time. Doing, what, though, I have no idea."

Her lips pursed. "I can think of one explanation. Nathan suggested it's possible he's a paranormal hunter."

"Hunter?" I echoed. "Hunting what, exactly?"

"Paranormal hunters are responsible for tracking down paranormals who break the rules," she explained. "Some work for the magical authorities, but most hunters belong to a regional collective. Nathan's family runs one branch in the northwest of England, but there are branches all around the country. If he's a freelancer, it makes sense for him not to settle down. Freelancers go where the work is."

"What exactly does a paranormal hunter do?" I asked. "I mean, can they use magic?"

"Generally, no," she said. "Paranormal hunters are usually born into families with a little magic but not enough that they can train as witches or wizards. That, or they're related to other hunters and get into it that way. Anyway, Nathan used to work for them, but he got fed up with the whole lifestyle. Some hunters aren't very nice to paranormals."

"So the two of them might have been hunting someone here?" Ivory Beach wasn't exactly a haven for paranormal criminals, but one of them *had* hidden in our library before the holidays. It wasn't outside the realm of possibility that both men had been on the same mission when they'd come here. Perhaps they'd needed the library's book for said mission, but if they didn't have magical talents of their own, they shouldn't have had any more luck at opening it than the rest of us did.

"Don't take my word for it," she said. "It's just a guess, but Nathan's good at recognising other hunters. Granted, I've never met one who dressed like a Death Eater before. Most of them dress like they're on a hiking trip."

I snorted. "I guess with those cloaks, they stand a better chance of blending in at this time of year."

"I can ask Nathan to speak to Mr Blake," she added. "He's more likely to talk to Nathan than to me, if he really is a hunter."

"Sure," I said. "Thanks for speaking to the others. I

appreciate it."

"No problem," she said.

I watched Blair leave the library, my thoughts spinning. If Mr Spencer had been a paranormal hunter, had he been hunting someone when he'd died? Mr Blake, too? Blair hadn't said what types of paranormals they hunted, but Mr Blake's reaction to Mr Dreyer's claim that he'd seen a vampire made more sense if he wanted to keep their mission a secret.

The image of Mortimer Vale appeared in my mind's eye, sending a violent shiver down my spine. Surely Evangeline would know if his fellow vampires were in town, and she'd send her own people to deal with it. I couldn't picture the leader of the vampires stepping back and letting humans do all the work, even people whose job was to hunt paranormal criminals.

Besides, Mr Dreyer's sighting outside the window didn't prove anything. For all we knew, the vampire had just been a curious local. Evangeline might even have sent one of her people to spy on the hotel's guests to make sure they behaved themselves. The only way to know for sure would be to talk to Evangeline herself, but she might not take kindly to me interrogating her.

The library door opened, and I scrambled to grab my wand. Then I let my hand drop, relief flooding me. It was only Edwin, flanked by his two troll guards. Despite their brutish appearances, one of them gave me a friendly wave and the other said, "Hey, Rory."

"Is something wrong?" I asked.

"Ah, Rory," said Edwin. "I'm told you have the book that Mr Spencer had in his possession shortly before he died."

"We do," I said. "That is—my aunt's dealing with it at the moment."

"I heard," he said. "There are rumours all over town. Is that the book which has been screaming and scaring off your patrons?"

Oops. In fairness, it was sort of hard *not* to hear the book screaming if you'd stepped into the library at any point in the last couple of days.

"I don't know if my aunts told you, but the book is giving us a bit of trouble," I said. "It has a sentience spell on it, but we haven't figured out how to get it to tell us if it knows more about Mr Spencer's death."

The elf blinked. "You're saying your family doesn't know how to open their own books?"

Well, when he put it like that… "I wasn't here when it was loaned out, so I can't really comment. Anyway, do you think the book might be linked to his death?"

"You said he mentioned it on the phone when he called you," said Edwin.

"He did, but as I said, we haven't been able to get any more information from the book itself," I said. "Have you spoken to Mr Blake, the other guest at the hotel? He and Mr Spencer knew one another, according to another guest came to visit the library. When I was giving her the tour, she mentioned that the two of them were both free-lancers in the same field."

His expression didn't change. "It's not so unusual for two people to want to get away to the sea for the holidays."

"Dressed in hooded cloaks which make them look like Death Eaters?" I raised an eyebrow.

Judging by his puzzled expression, he didn't get the

reference. "It's not my place to judge. I've questioned all the guests, and so far, the one puzzling element remains that book."

"That's why I wondered if you'd spoken to Mr Blake," I said. "I'm sure the book itself knows more than it's letting on, too." I figured that perhaps if he knew we had good reason to be involved, he'd be more open to sharing information with me. After all, the book *did* know something about Mr Spencer's death. I was sure of it.

"The book?" he said. "Are you saying it might have communicated with the victim before his death?" His tone dripped with scepticism. The elf policeman might deal with more than his average share of strangeness, but it seemed a sentient book was a step too far.

"It's under a sentience spell, so maybe. That is, if he knew how to get it to stop screaming," I said. "Also, I was just talking to Blair—she's staying at the hotel, too—and she said one of the guests spotted a vampire outside the window last night."

"A vampire?" he said. "Who, exactly?"

I shook my head. "No clue. The guest's from out of town, so he wouldn't know any of Evangeline's people on sight, but he said the man moved as fast as a vampire would."

His brows climbed into his hairline. "Did this so-called vampire act suspicious in any way?"

"Other than peering through windows?" I said. "Uh, have you heard from Mortimer Vale lately?"

"Heard from him?" he echoed. "He's still in jail, and he seems utterly disinterested in the outside world. He knows he's in there for life, after all."

"I was just wondering, since one of the guests saw a

vampire, and his two friends were never caught…"

"Rory," he said. His tone wasn't unkind. "I've been in some tough situations in my time as head of the police here, and I understand where your fear is coming from. But you're going to have to learn to work through it."

Shame shot through me like a bolt of lightning. He thought I was letting my fear of vampires cloud my judgement, and perhaps I was, but I didn't see why anyone would lie about seeing a strange vampire hanging around the hotel. Their alarming speed made them difficult to mistake for an ordinary person, too.

"I am," I told him. "That's not what I meant. I just thought you might want to know what Blair told me."

"Well, tell your aunt to find me if she manages to get any more information from that book," he said. "If the book *does* count as a witness, we'll have to take it in."

"Believe me, you might not like that," I warned. "Unless you have soundproofed cells, that is. I'll let you know if we find anything."

"Thank you, Rory."

I watched him leave, followed by his troll guards, and wished I could make him understand it wasn't my fear of vampires alone that made me suspicious of their involvement. In fairness, it wasn't hard to see why he'd come to that conclusion. I'd be more inclined to believe I was acting out of my fear of vampires than that there was a rogue in town, considering Mr Dreyer hadn't reported the sighting to the police himself.

Annoyance prickled at me, more directed at my own fear than anything else. I wasn't the same person I'd been when I'd first run into Mortimer Vale, and besides, whether they were involved with Mr Spencer's death or not, it was about time I took my relationship with the vampires into my own hands.

Once I was free for my lunch hour, I left the library and walked into the town square, angling towards the road that led uphill to the vampires' home. I made it all the way to the church before second thoughts started to kick in. Maybe I'd been a little hasty. Maybe… oh, no.

Evangeline stood outside the doors, for all the world like she'd been waiting for me the whole time. She couldn't have read my mind from all the way over in the library, but she did seem to have an unnerving instinct for figuring me out. Unless she'd heard about the vampire Mr Dreyer had seen at the hotel through another source, that is.

I halted a few feet away from her. "Hello, Evangeline."

"Hello, Aurora," she said. "Is there a reason you wanted to speak to me?

Well, I let my irritation at Edwin thinking I was being paranoid and not rational convince me to come here to talk to you, and now I'm having second thoughts.

I kept my attention on the pavement, trying not to let those thoughts slip into the forefront of my mind where she could read them. Instead, I said, "You tell me."

She chuckled. "You're getting bolder. I know you're looking for information, and I assumed curiosity would lead you to ask me. I'm aware of your friend Blair and her talent for getting to the truth."

Great. How'd she even found that out? She must have read it from someone's mind, though I didn't have the impression Blair shared that information with everyone she met. Her gleaming eyes invited me to step closer, but I didn't move. Keeping my distance from her made little difference considering her ability to move at an inhuman speed, but it made me feel more at ease.

"Then you must also know that there's no information I can't get from anyone, via her talent," I said. "She knows if anyone is lying."

"Ah, but that's not the same as having access to someone's inmost thoughts," she said. "Though I confess, I don't need to be a mind-reader to access certain information. I've lived in this town a long time, Rory, and I've seen many people come and go. You should know that Mr Spencer was married once, and his ex-wife still lives here in Ivory Beach."

Whatever I'd expected her to say, it wasn't that. "Really? He was married?"

"Why do you humans insist on repeating my words back to me?"

"Because we don't get to hear people's thoughts before they speak," I said. "Did she even know he was in town?"

"Considering she was the last person whose number he dialled before he called the library?" she said. "Yes, she did."

"How did you—" I didn't need to ask. She'd read it from someone's mind. Frederick's, maybe, since he was the one who'd picked up Mr Spencer's phone after his death.

Argh. Why does she have to be like this? Never mind my rational fear of vampires—at this rate, they were going to exasperate me into an early grave without any fangs being involved.

"Evangeline?" said a voice from beside my shoulder. "Why are you talking to Rory?"

Xavier. How long had he been standing there? He was

as stealthy as any vampire, that was for sure.

"Why, nothing," said Evangeline. "Such *accusations*, Reaper. I'll be going now."

Between one blink and the next, she'd vanished, only the faint movement of the church door closing betraying that she'd been here at all. So much for asking if she knew if there were any rogues in town.

"Rory?" said Xavier. "Did you come here to talk to her?"

"Yes," I said shortly. "And I think we ought to move away from her door because she can hear every word we say."

Why had she told me about Mr Spencer's ex-wife? Perhaps she'd been intending to distract me from asking about vampire rogues, but the fact that he'd called his ex-wife before his death sounded like something the police needed to know, if they didn't already.

Xavier gave me a sideways frown. "Why did you want to talk to her?"

"About Mr Spencer's death," I said. "I thought the vampires might be involved, except when I came here to talk to her, she dropped another bombshell on my head."

"Which is...?"

"Mr Spencer was married once," I said. "To a woman who still lives here in Ivory Beach. She also claimed he called her the day he died. Or possibly the other way around."

"We can check," he said. "If she called him, she knew he was here, but it depends if he was the one to make the call."

"And if she answered," I added. "Either way, I think we need to question his ex-wife."

8

Xavier and I walked to the library together. I half expected Evangeline to make a reappearance behind us and ask about the screaming book again, but she didn't. Silence spread between Xavier and me, filling with questions about how on earth he'd known where I was. The Reapers' home wasn't far from where the vampires hung out, true, but to be honest, I still didn't know how he spent the time he wasn't looking for souls to escort into the next world.

"I assume the police know," said Xavier. "About Mr Spencer's wife, I mean."

"Not necessarily." I forced my thoughts back to the present. "He seems to have made a career out of making himself impossible to find. My aunts had to spend days researching before they found out where he'd been for the last few years, let alone where he actually came from. And they didn't mention anything about marriage. I should have asked Evangeline for more details, but I was shocked she told me anything at all."

"Are you sure she's being truthful?"

"If she is, I bet she gave me that information for a reason," I said. "She's playing a game with me."

His forehead scrunched up in concern. "Vampire games aren't worth the risk."

"But if they could help us catch a killer?" I said. "I don't know what else to do. Blair talked to the guests and it sounds like one of them saw a vampire last night, outside his hotel room."

"Blair?"

I told him about my two encounters with Blair. I hoped she wouldn't mind me mentioning her lie-sensing abilities, but she'd told me about them during her first meeting and Xavier was good at keeping secrets. Too good, if anything.

"So you showed this Blair around the library?" he asked.

"Not all of it," I said. "You can't fit a tour of the whole library into a year, let alone an hour."

He gave me a smile. "Just the highlights, then."

"Yeah." I was such a hopeless case. He'd ditched me once already, and his boss hated my guts, and yet the instant he smiled, I melted, a fact which probably said more about my sanity than any visit to the vampires did.

Giving myself a mental shake, I pushed open the door to the library and found Estelle at the front desk.

Her eyes bulged at the sight of Xavier. "Hey. I thought you left town."

"I came back." He shot me a questioning look, as though wondering why I hadn't told my family about him. "I heard you were researching Mr Spencer's history."

Estelle's brow wrinkled. "Yes, but I didn't think you

were involved in the case. Or are you? Is that why you came back?"

"Not exactly," he said. "But Rory found out something more."

"He used to be married," I explained. "His ex-wife lives here in town, but we don't know her name or address. Edwin might, but he already spoke to me today and he'll get annoyed if I start pestering him."

"I'll tell my mum," she said. "Can you watch the desk?"

"Sure." I walked behind the counter, and Xavier followed. "You don't have to wait here."

"Of course I do," he said. "I'm sticking with this for as long as you are, Rory."

Why? He'd barely returned to town, and we still hadn't dealt with the oh-so-slightly important issue of the Grim Reaper's disapproval. If he'd been following the rules, his involvement ought to have ended after he'd escorted the guy's soul into the afterlife, but I kept my fingers crossed that the Grim Reaper stayed out of this one.

Sylvester flew down to land on the logbook. "So you brought the Reaper here again, did you?"

"There you are," I said to the owl. "I assumed the book had eaten you."

He let out a disdainful hoot. "That pathetic excuse for a book is nothing compared to me."

"Really, you two have a lot in common," I said. "Are you sure you aren't first cousins?"

The owl ruffled his wings in a threatening manner. "Are you sure you want to keep all your fingers?"

I rolled my eyes. "I could have told my family there's an easy way to find out how to read the book, you know." Namely, the Forbidden Room. Even Xavier didn't know

Sylvester's true nature, but I was never entirely sure if the owl's threats were serious.

The owl huffed. "If you think I can get that book open, you're wasting your time."

"Wait, you can't *open* the book?" said Xavier. "I thought you knew everything about all the books in the library."

"Did I ever make that claim?" the owl enquired.

"Yes," I said. "Multiple times. Anyway, the book is under a sentience spell and neither of my aunts has managed to get it open."

"This ridiculous matter is no longer worth my time." Sylvester spread his wings, took flight, and disappeared over the bookcases.

"Yeah, right," I said. "He doesn't want to admit he's stumped, too. The book went out on a long-term loan, so Mr Spencer might have borrowed it years ago for all we know."

"And now it turns out he was married," said Xavier. "You don't think he might have come to Ivory Beach to see his ex-wife?"

"Maybe, but he was cutting it pretty close to the deadline to return the book," I said. "The book was rigged to screaming if it wasn't returned on time. Though it screams the rest of the time, too."

"But your friend managed to speak to it?" he asked.

"Who—oh, Blair," I said. "Not for long enough to learn anything substantial. The book clammed up the instant it figured out she could tell truth from lie. I think we need to get creative if we want answers."

Estelle returned, crossing the lobby towards us. "You're right," she said. "Mr Spencer was married to a woman called Lauren, who changed back to her maiden name, Peterson, after their divorce five years ago. They were only married for two years, and it looks like Mr Spencer was still doing the nomad thing then, so I have no idea how that worked out."

"Do you have an address?" I asked.

"Lauren works at the local antique shop," said Estelle. "It's open today, so if you want to head over there, she should be there."

"It's worth checking out." I glanced at Xavier. "If he called her the day he died, it'll be for a reason. We can just check into the shop for a look around. It's not like we're paying a social call."

"True," he acknowledged. "Okay, let's go."

I led the way out of the library again, hoping I wasn't making a mistake in following Evangeline's advice. That vampire was as much of a mystery as Mr Spencer, if not more, which was no doubt exactly how she wanted everyone to see her. And while she'd offered me the information freely, I wouldn't put it past her to call in a favour at a later date.

The antique shop was located down a side street off the town square. We entered through the red-painted door to find a small room crammed with various odds and ends, all of which looked centuries old. An ancient cuckoo clock sang at the wall beside a spinning disk of coloured lights, an innocuous-looking armchair turned into what looked like a medieval torture device as we passed by, and several bloodstained instruments filled one shelf marked with names. I wasn't entirely sure if the names belonged to their previous owners or their victims.

A middle-aged woman with tightly curled dark hair

sat behind the counter. She must be Mrs Spencer—no, Peterson.

"Hello," she said, her eyes widening a little in surprise. "You're the Reaper, aren't you? It's not my time, is it?"

"Not yet." I didn't think he *meant* to sound creepy, but he must know hearing those words from a Reaper wasn't exactly reassuring.

The woman's eyes flew wider. "I suppose that's good news, then. Looking for anything in particular?"

"Uh, we actually wanted to talk to you," I said, opting for the direct approach. Without Blair's lie-sensing power, I couldn't dance around the subject and still ensure I got the right information. "About your ex-husband."

Her expression shadowed. "What about him?"

"I heard you spoke on the phone," I said. "Not long before he died."

"How did you—?" She looked from Xavier to me. "I suppose Howard's phone is in the police's hands, though few people knew we were married. But yes… he called me the other morning before he died."

"Any particular reason?" I asked.

"I didn't answer the phone. I was in the shower." She shook her head. "I suppose I'll never know what he wanted to say to me, but it didn't seem right to push myself into the investigation when we hadn't seen one another face to face in years. After all…"

"They might suspect you?" said Xavier.

"Of what?" Her hands clenched on the counter, her knuckles whitening. "Do the police think his death wasn't an accident?"

"They think there was something odd about the

timing," I said carefully. "My family owns the library, and he returned one of our books shortly before his death."

"I'm afraid I don't know about any books," she said. "But I imagine he must have wanted to call and say hello to me before he left town. After all, it's been a few years, and we were good friends for a while after our divorce."

Hmm. Wishing I had Blair with me to verify if she spoke the truth, I went on. "What did he do for a living?"

"It's not really my place to tell you."

I'd suspected not. "He was a freelance paranormal hunter, right? Did he ever deal with vampires?"

From the blank shock on her face, I'd guessed right. Xavier shot me a brief sideways look, then turned back to Mrs Peterson. "That's why he moved around so much? He was a freelance hunter?"

"Yes, he was." Her shoulders slumped. "He'd be annoyed with me for telling you, but I suppose it doesn't matter at this point. When we married, he claimed he planned to retire, but he found it hard to stop taking on freelance cases. Eventually, it drove us apart. I mean, who wants to wake up to find a note from their spouse saying they've gone to kill a rogue vampire in the middle of the night?" She chuckled and shook her head.

"Didn't you know his history?" I asked. "I mean, he must have told you what he did for a living before you married."

"He led me to believe he'd turned over a new leaf," she said. "He was obsessive, though. Sometimes he'd use my contacts in the world of antiques to work out an angle to get at a vampire, and then forget I existed the rest of the time when he was working a case. Eventually, I moved out. It took him a week to notice."

"Ah," I said. "So—did you live here together? In Ivory Beach, I mean?"

"No," she said. "We originally met in London, and I thought we'd stay, but even when we lived in the same city, he took frequent trips outside for work. Any hint of a rumour about a rogue and he was gone."

"And what about other vampire hunters?" I asked. "Like Mr Blake? He claimed it was a coincidence that he and your ex-husband showed up in town at the same time, but I'm guessing they worked in the same profession. Were they friends?"

"I'm not sure Howard *had* friends," she said. "It was a dangerous profession and I didn't blame him for his paranoia, but it got out of hand by the end. He saw enemies everywhere."

"But did you know Mr Blake?" asked Xavier.

"I wouldn't say we knew one another," she said. "I heard Howard mention his name a few times. I got the impression the two of them were rivals before they quit hunting."

Rivals? Was that why they'd argued the morning of Mr Spencer's death? If the two had been after the same target, perhaps they hadn't been working together after all. But that was pure conjecture.

The question was, why had Evangeline told me about Mr Spencer's ex-wife to begin with? You'd think she'd be more concerned with his vampire-hunting history, even if he only went after rogue paranormals.

And what of the book? Did it contain some top-secret vampire-related information? Maybe that's why it was so cagey about sharing its secrets.

"Okay," I said. "Thanks for talking to us. If you find

anything out about that book, can you let me or my aunts know? We'd appreciate it."

"I will," she said. "I hope you get your answers."

I left the shop, steering clear of the cursed-looking chair and trying my best not to look at the bloody instruments on the shelves.

"So Blair was right," I murmured. "Mr Spencer and Mr Blake were both vampire hunters. If Mr Blake didn't kill him, a vampire might have. The vampire they were both hunting."

"I don't know," said Xavier. "Pushing someone downstairs? Not really a vampire thing. They tend to go for the neck."

"That'd be too obvious, though." I shivered. "Think about how fast and quietly they move. It'd have been easy for one to sneak into the hotel and push him downstairs without being caught."

"Normally I'd agree, but I assume former vampire hunters are wise to their tricks and constantly watch their backs," said Xavier. "If he survived for years as a freelance vampire hunter, he couldn't have easily let his guard down."

"True," I acknowledged. "Edwin thinks I'm letting my paranoia get the best of me, but I'm not even the first one to bring up vampires. One of the other guests saw a vampire from his window in the middle of the night."

"Edwin said what?" The surprise in his voice gratified me, though my cheeks stung with renewed humiliation. "You have reason to be wary, yes, but there's more than one connection between vampires and this case."

"We know that now," I said. "I can't believe my family missed the ex-wife in their research."

"Speaking of whom," he said. "Didn't you tell your family I was back in town?"

Uh... Now I was blushing for a different reason entirely. "It never came up. I wasn't sure you weren't about to leave again, anyway."

I'd spent the last two weeks trying to forget him, but the lack of closure had stung the most. It was much easier to move on if you knew what you were moving on from.

"I already told you," he said. "I said I won't disappear this time, and I meant it."

"But you're still not allowed to see me," I said. "From that note, it sounded like your boss meant business." To say the least.

"Did he say anything to you in person?" His voice was uncharacteristically hesitant.

I shook my head. "No, but the fact that he went to the trouble of leaving me a personal note telling me never to contact you again was pretty clear. Has he found out we've spoken since?"

"You haven't broken your word," he said. "I contacted you, not the other way around. He's rarely spoken to me since my return to town, and he has no interest in what the two of us do together."

I had my doubts. Even if Xavier *did* plan to stick around, spending every one of our dates dodging the Grim Reaper was no plan for a long-term relationship. "Even talking to Evangeline?"

I was tempted to go looking for her again to ask if she knew what Mr Spencer had done for a living. Maybe I should take Blair along, too, but I didn't know if her lie-sensing ability even worked on vampires. Besides, she'd come here for a holiday, not to play mind games with the leader of the vampires.

"I won't mention that part to him," said Xavier. "He isn't a fan of the vampires."

"Then it sounds like he wouldn't want you involved in this case, though," I said. "Unless he knows you took Mr Spencer's soul to the afterlife?"

"He doesn't," he said. "I deal with a lot of souls, and he has no interested in who they were in life."

"I bet not." Personally, I'd much rather be escorted into the afterlife by a golden-haired angel of death than a cold and terrifying inhuman figure in a hooded cloak, but the dead didn't get to pick and choose. "I guess if you chat with the dead on a daily basis…" I trailed off as Xavier's body froze, his gaze fixed somewhere in the distance. "What is it?"

His expression turned serious. "I'm being called to pick up another soul."

My heart lurched. "But—"

He moved forwards, the scythe suddenly in his hands, and the next instant he was *gone.* I spotted his blond head vanishing down the road by the clock tower and sprinted that way, my breath coming in sharp gasps. After weeks of working at the library, I was in the best shape I'd been in my life, but no human could keep up with a Reaper on the hunt. He moved like a ghost, a flicker of light moving across town.

Then, he stopped, his scythe held high above his head.

I skidded to a halt outside the hotel, where the crumpled body of Mr Blake lay spread-eagled on the pavement. A gasp rose in my throat as shadows fanned out from Xavier's body, engulfing the area until darkness smothered my surroundings. Within the darkness, a door appeared, edged in light which shone against the surrounding shadows. I inched closer, but in another instant, the ghostly figure of Mr Blake passed through the door and was gone.

Xavier lowered the scythe. His expression was as grim as his namesake as the shadows vanished, leaving nothing behind but Mr Blake's lifeless body.

9

I came back to my senses when the hotel doors opened, the guests spilling out to stare and gasp at the scene, while passers-by from the nearby streets hurried over to take a look.

"You again?" said Frederick. "Aurora—don't tell me *he* called your library, too."

"I was with the Reaper when he ran here," I said, still breathless from my sprint across town. "How—how did he die?"

"Looks like he jumped," someone said.

All eyes went to the window, three floors up, which was wide open, swaying in the cold breeze coming off the seafront.

"Damn," Frederick murmured. "Everyone—step away, now. I'm going to call the police."

I edged closer to Xavier, only too keen to leave the body and head down the side street alongside the clock tower.

"Weird for a vampire," I muttered to Xavier. "I thought they only ever bit their victims."

Then again, they didn't typically commit murder in broad daylight, either. Now it'd happened twice in the same place.

"I don't think anything is off-limits when it comes to vampires," he said quietly.

No kidding. Now both people who might know the truth about Mr Spencer's death were dead.

Blair detached herself from the crowd and approached me. "I don't know if it matters now," she said in a low voice, "but Nathan did have the chance to talk to Mr Blake this morning. He asked if he was a vampire hunter."

"We got it confirmed," I said, my voice hollow. "From his ex-wife. Both he and Mr Spencer used to be vampire hunters. Rivals, she said."

Nathan stepped up to Blair's side. "He wasn't an active hunter," he said. "He quit freelancing years ago. He clammed up when he realised I was grilling him for information."

"Thanks anyway," I said. "We… we were actually on our way here to speak to him, but it looks like someone else got here first."

Both he and Mr Spencer might have quit hunting vampires, but how had they ended up picking the same holiday destination and then been killed? Two dead ex-vampire hunters in the space of a week couldn't be an accident however you looked at it.

"Did you say his ex-wife?" asked Blair. "I didn't know he was married."

"Neither did I until today," I said. "They divorced five

years ago, and she went back to using her maiden name afterwards. She works in the town's antique shop."

I debated telling her about Evangeline, but she and Nathan had had enough to deal with without meeting the terrifying leader of the vampires. I wouldn't blame them if they never wanted to come back to Ivory Beach again.

"Hey…" Blair peered up at Mr Blake's window. "He was on the third floor? Why were you up there, then?"

I turned to see who she addressed and found myself face to face with Mr Dreyer, the relic hunter. He blanched. "Me?"

"Yes," said Blair. "When Nathan and I were out earlier, I looked up and saw you in his room through the window. You're staying on the first floor, same as us. I know you are."

"What were you doing in Mr Blake's room?" asked Nathan.

He opened and closed his mouth. "Why… you must have been mistaken."

Blair twitched. "You're lying."

"I'm not—"

"Better to talk to me than to the police," said Blair. "Tell me the truth. Why were you in his room?"

His shoulders slumped. "He kept dropping hints the other day about looking in town for something valuable, so I wanted to see if he had it in his room."

"Really," said Nathan, his voice flat. "Are you sure you didn't push him out the window when his back was turned?"

"No," he insisted. "I had a look around and then left. That's all. I swear."

Blair shook her head. "Best of luck trying that one on the police."

Mr Dreyer paled. "I'm not… I didn't push him."

I caught Blair's eye and she shook her head a little. Did that mean he was telling the truth—or lying?

"I'm afraid I'll have to ask you to leave." Frederick nodded to Xavier and me. "Both of you."

"Was he lying?" I whispered to Blair.

"No," she returned. "But he's no saint, that's for sure."

The relic hunter was the only possible suspect who wasn't a vampire or connected to them, and he hadn't specified *what* he'd been searching for in Mr Blake's room.

"Reaper?" said Frederick. "You're done here, yes?"

"I am." Xavier stepped back, away from the crime scene. "I have to check in with my boss and let him know."

I walked with him down the street. "You won't tell him we planned to speak to Mr Blake ourselves?"

"Of course not," he said. "The less he knows about this, the better."

I had to agree with him there. But how was it possible to keep the Grim Reaper out of our business when people kept showing up dead?

———

"What's wrong?" asked Cass, when I re-entered the library to find her staffing the desk. "Did you and the Reaper break up again? Joking, joking," she added, as Estelle shot her a warning look.

"Cass, that really isn't funny," said Estelle. "Rory, what is it?"

"Mr Blake is dead." I heaved out a breath. "I need to speak to Aunt Adelaide."

"Here," said my aunt, approaching with an armful of books. "Is the Reaper back in town?"

"Funny, I thought she'd be telling everyone." Cass shut her mouth when I glared at her.

"Xavier and I talked to Mr Spencer's ex-wife and she told us that both he and Mr Blake were retired vampire hunters," I explained. "We went to the hotel to question Mr Blake, but he was dead. I think someone pushed him out the window."

The others quietened as I explained the day's events. Even Cass stopped making snarky comments to listen to me.

"So you know the two of them were vampire hunters," said Cass. "And now they're both dead. Is it not obvious who killed them? Or rather, *what* killed them?"

"If a vampire is responsible, we have no clues as to their identity," I pointed out. "Also, Mr Dreyer was seen snooping around in Mr Blake's room earlier today. He claimed to have nothing to do with his death, but for all we know, he knows more than he's letting on. It's anyone's guess at this point."

"Both men were active vampire hunters?" Aunt Adelaide frowned. "Are you sure? Because they'd be required to disclose that information upon entering the town. It's in our rules."

"They were retired," I said. "Not sure if that'd show up on any records or not, but Blair's boyfriend is a former paranormal hunter and he talked to Mr Blake and confirmed it before his death."

"Who is Blair?" said Cass.

"Blair's another guest at the hotel," I told her. "She came for a tour around the library the other day. Anyway, she's talked to most of the suspects by now. Except for the ex-wife, but we only found out she existed this morning. She's the one who told us that Mr Spencer used to be a vampire hunter."

"None of the town's vampires would be bothered by an ex-vampire hunter from outside the town visiting," said Aunt Adelaide. "So if a vampire *was* responsible—"

"If?" Cass snorted. "You know those vampires are centuries old and have long memories, right? If it were me, and they killed one of my friends, I'd want revenge."

Estelle raised an eyebrow. "Do you want to tell Evangeline that?"

I had an inkling I'd missed a couple of family arguments while I'd been questioning suspects and showing Blair around. "I'm not talking to her until I know for sure. One of the guests saw a vampire outside the window the other night as well, but they didn't get a close enough look to be able to describe who it was."

Aunt Adelaide's lips pressed together. "Unless they gave an accurate description, it would be difficult to prove."

"Yeah, well, both of them are dead now," said Cass. "Which is tragic and everything, but the vampires have had their revenge. We should let it go."

"And if the book was involved?" I said. "What if the vampires are after the book, too?"

Cass made a sceptical noise. "Yeah, right. The book's been in the library for years before the vampire hunters ever showed up."

"Don't forget Mr Spencer's last phone call was to the library, and he mentioned the book," I reminded her.

"Which proves what?" Cass said. "By all means, let Aunt Candace waste her time screwing around with that ridiculous book if it distracts her from taking notes on me to use in her stories. But don't drag our family into any more drama."

I frowned at her. "Aren't you in the least bit worried that there's a book here in the library none of us can read, which might be hiding clues about two murders?"

"No. There are a lot of books in here nobody can read."

"But not involved in murder cases," Estelle interjected. "I'm with Rory. This is still our business, and we have to at least prepare for the possibility of the police showing up here to question us as well."

"They didn't have much to say last time," I said. "Poor Frederick is going to take the backlash, in all likelihood, but two ex-vampire hunters dying in mysterious accidents in the space of a week? Even the police will have to admit there's something off there."

"We will wait and see what Edwin says," said Aunt Adelaide. "In the meantime, I notice there's a number of returns that haven't been dealt with. Cass, you start on those. Rory, can I have a word with you?"

As Cass picked up the box, grumbling, Aunt Adelaide beckoned me aside. "If you want me to give the translator spell a try on your dad's journal, it's back in working order."

My heart gave a nervous flip. "Really?"

"If you're sure," she said.

I reached into my bag and handed her the journal. "I am. I'm just surprised it's an option."

"It's a tremendously difficult spell," she said. "It's lucky it still works after Candace tried to use it to translate the title of that wretched book."

"If the vampires are hunting for the journal, it can't be impossible to read, right?" I said. "There wouldn't be much value in its information if it was."

"I suppose not," she said. "But if you're worried about that particular group of vampires, I doubt they're involved in the recent murders. They're far too ancient and clever to draw the attention of rogue vampire hunters. I'm more inclined to believe someone had a grudge against both men and targeted them when they were in the same place. If the book is involved, it's tangential at best."

"The relic hunter guy seemed pretty unscrupulous, whether he's the killer or not," I added. "He sneaked into Mr Blake's room in broad daylight to have a nose around and see if he had any rare artefacts in his room. That's not the act of an innocent man."

"No, but he knows neither of the two men had the book at the time of their deaths," said Aunt Adelaide. "Why not come to the library if that's what he wanted to find?"

"Maybe he didn't," I said. "Unless… we never did have the chance to ask Mr Blake if *he* knew how to open the book."

Cass loudly cleared her throat from beside the front desk. "Someone's here."

I turned around to find Xavier was back in the library, scythe and all. That must have been a quick meeting with the Grim Reaper.

"Well, well," said Cass. "The Reaper really is back in town."

"Hello, Cass," said Xavier. "I'm here—"

"To see Rory?"

Aunt Adelaide stepped in. "Oh—hello, Reaper. I didn't know you were back."

"He's here because he was called to collect the souls of the two victims," I said, for Cass's benefit. "That's how I ended up at the murder scene."

"Convenient," said Cass, and Estelle elbowed her in the ribs.

"Nice to see you," Estelle said to him.

"Likewise," he said. "I wonder if I could trouble you for a peek at that book of yours?"

"I suppose Rory told you about it." Aunt Adelaide glanced over her shoulder. "Candace seems to have taken it upon herself to crack the code. It's giving her considerable trouble, but perhaps you'll be able to get some sense out of it."

"More than Rory," said Cass, with a smirk.

"Cass!" Estelle said. "What is the matter with you today?"

"Oh, the usual," said Cass. "You know most people don't have the Reaper showing up on the doorstep on a weekly basis? We run into more dead bodies than the people who work in the mortuary."

"Xavier hasn't been here in weeks," I pointed out.

"Oh, we know *that.*" Cass winced as Estelle stood on her foot. Hard.

"Cass, behave," said Aunt Adelaide. "I'll tell Candace. Estelle, can you deal with the returns? Make sure Cass does her fair share."

"Sure," said Estelle. "Sylvester?"

The owl swooped down. "What is it this time? I was napping."

Feeling slightly guilty for skipping out on helping Estelle deal with the returns *and* Cass in a temper, I walked with Xavier back through the Reading Corner to wait for Aunt Candace.

"Sorry about them," I said. "If you wanted to leave town because of my annoying family, I wouldn't blame you at this point."

He grinned. "No. Honestly, I've missed this."

"Missed what? Cass being Cass, Sylvester being irritating, or books that bite fingers instead of answering questions?"

"You, of course."

My throat clogged with all the words I wanted to say, but I could just imagine Aunt Candace preparing her notebook on the other side of the door. I cast my mind around for a change of subject. "So—do you have any Reaper tricks for opening that book without it screaming, biting, or turning itself inside-out and showing only blank pages?"

He frowned. "Can't you contact the publisher or the author? Or the person who put the spell on the book to begin with?"

"You'd think so, but my grandmother wasn't exactly meticulous at keeping track of details," I said. "There are plenty of books in here which are one of a kind, so we have nothing to compare them to."

"You think the killer might be after the book, then?"

"Maybe," I said. "If both victims were killed by the same vampire, it wouldn't have been hard for them to find out the book was here in the library after the first death. Besides, we're losing business because of its screaming and temper tantrums."

Xavier glanced at the closed door. "Is there any known link between that relic hunter and the two victims, then? Anything to suggest he might have been following them?"

"Pretty sure only the police know, if at all." I shook my head. "If the book would just *talk*, then we'd know if we have any reason to worry about it."

"Did Mr Spencer know how to handle it, then?" he asked.

"He knew its habit of screaming," I said. "He also had it in his possession for months or years, though, so he must have found a way to keep it from screaming the place down. Unless he kept it in a locked room. But if vampires were hunting him, it wouldn't exactly have helped him keep a low profile."

"Do you think they were looking for the book?"

"I honestly don't know," I admitted. "I mean, why would he bring it back here, knowing they were hunting him? He might at least have warned us first."

"Maybe that's why he called you."

Perhaps he did. But the vampires had got there first.

Aunt Candace opened the door. "The book is ready for you. Good luck, Reaper."

I turned to Xavier. "Want to meet the screaming book?"

10

The book remained deceptively still and quiet when we entered the room. Xavier took the lead, leaning over the table to examine the book's cover.

"Hello to you too," the book said.

To give Xavier credit, he didn't jump. "So are you sentient or under a spell?"

"What are *you*, then?" said the book. "Not a wizard."

"Not quite." He picked up the book and turned it over in his hands to look at the back cover.

"Put me down, you rude little—"

"Hey!" I said to the book.

"Oh, it's you again." The book let out a dramatic sigh. "Are you passing me among all your friends now?"

"Yes," I said. "You should know Mr Blake was murdered today."

"Am I supposed to care?"

"So you do know who he is?" said Xavier.

"Did I say so?"

"You ask a lot of questions for someone who's meant to have answers." Xavier flipped over the book again. "Is there a secret password to get in here?"

"What?" squawked the book.

"Wait, *is* there?" I said. "Is that the key?"

"There is no key," said the book.

I wish Blair was here. Why hadn't I thought to ask that question before? A secret password would explain the book's refusal to share any information. If we found it, we might just have cracked the book's secrets.

Xavier put the book down. "Two people were murdered who had contact with you in the last week. Both were former vampire hunters. Were you aware?"

"It's not like I make a habit of talking to every human who picks me up and manhandles me," said the book. "*You*, though. You're not quite human. What are you?"

"I'm the Reaper," he said, matter-of-factly.

"An angel of death?" said the book. "What does the angel of death want with me, I wonder?"

"I'd like you to cooperate with me and share what you know." His tone was clear, his words precise.

"You think I'll cooperate?" the book said in petulant tones. "The cheek of it. You accuse me of being involved in two murders and then expect me to open for you. You won't take *my* soul, angel of death."

"Probably because you don't have one," I said. "Um, it doesn't, does it?"

"It doesn't," confirmed Xavier. "If it did, I'd be able to sense it."

Unfortunately, it didn't seem to have a key, either. Xavier and I spent fifteen minutes trying to open it before the book started another screaming fit, at which point we left the room and closed the door.

Luckily, someone had soundproofed the room, and the noise didn't follow us into the library.

I rubbed my temples. "I have no idea if the book was just messing with me again then, or if it really could arrange my death if it wanted to." As if I needed another reason to be paranoid.

Xavier gave the closed door a dark look. "Your family are the ones who purchased the book, are they not? They wouldn't have done so if it posed a real threat to them."

"I'm starting to think someone dumped it on them, to be honest." I shook my head. "Well, it's worth telling my Aunt Adelaide that the book might require a password to activate. I would have thought Aunt Candace might have already tried it, but she tends to go for the complicated solution rather than the easy one."

With nothing left to try, we walked to the front desk to find Cass sitting there alone.

"You're too late," said Cass, in sullen tones. "My mum's gone to speak to the police. So has Estelle."

"Why?" I said. "About the murder?"

"No, about her bad leg. Of course it's about the bloody murder. Or murders. Does everyone you talk to drop dead?"

"You tell me," I said.

Xavier gave a stifled laugh, hastily cut off at the expression on Cass's face. "Some of us don't need her help."

Now I was the one to laugh. I'd like to set *her* against the Grim Reaper. That would be interesting to watch. Or terrifying.

"Hilarious," said Cass. "What do you want with my mum?"

"I was going to ask her to convince Edwin to let us look at Mr Spencer's possessions, assuming they were removed from his room," I explained. "That way, we might be able to see if *he* knew how to open the book. If there was a secret password, he must have written that down, too."

"A password?" Cass's brow furrowed. "The book has a password?"

"The book acted shady when we brought up the subject, and it's one of the few things we haven't tried yet," I said. "Has Aunt Candace tried, do you know?"

"I guess not, but I can ask her. Anything that gets the bloody thing out of our hair by this point."

She walked out from behind the desk and headed for the family living quarters, leaving me blinking after her. "You're welcome," she said over her shoulder.

Since when did Cass volunteer to do anything? Maybe Estelle had given her a stern talking-to after their earlier arguments. That, or she was as keen to get rid of the book as the rest of us.

"She's being even more Jekyll and Hyde than usual," I said to Xavier. "Earlier, she was giving me endless grief about our getting tangled in another murder case, and now she's being nice instead."

"You mean, I got you tangled in the murder case," he said. "Occupational hazard of spending time with a Reaper, I'm afraid."

"Nah, Mr Spencer is the one who kicked this off," I said. "I doubt I'll ever find out what it is he wanted to tell me when he called me. Now we're stuck with a screaming book for the long haul."

"That explains why there aren't any patrons around," Xavier commented.

Now I looked around, Xavier and I were alone in the reception area. The air thickened with tension as the memory of dancing with him right here in the lobby infiltrated my mind. I remembered kissing him, thinking I couldn't possibly be happier—right before the Grim Reaper showed up and ruined everything.

"Rory?" he said. "You look like you have a lot on your mind, aside from the obvious."

I'd never been good at hiding my thoughts, but it wouldn't do any good to remind either of us of what we couldn't have. I cast my gaze around for a distraction and spotted the translator spell sitting on the desk. "Ah. I asked my aunt to put my dad's journal in here to see if we could get a translation."

The box glowed faintly green around the edges, and it sprang open when I picked it up. The journal was intact, thankfully, but the lone blank page that came out along with it was covered in indecipherable markings.

"Oh." My shoulders slumped. "It didn't work."

"What is that?" Xavier peered at the box.

"A translator spell my Aunt Adelaide was working on." I slipped my dad's journal back into my bag. "I guess it doesn't work if there's no translation available. Which is bad news for me, but also bad news for the vampires who want to steal it, too."

"The vampires," he repeated. "Do you think there might be a link between that group of vampires and this case?"

"My aunt didn't seem to think so," I said. "But if there is a rogue vampire in town, they're still at large, and either Evangeline doesn't know, or she doesn't care."

"If she knew, she'd care," he said, with certainty. "Did she drop any hints when you spoke to her?"

"Nope, but she did want to borrow the book," I said. "I said no, because it was screaming. She wouldn't say why she was interested in it, but I haven't heard her mention vampires or rogues or anything. Even when I went to see her, all she did was point me towards Mr Spencer's ex-wife."

"Yes, you went to see her," he said. "You must know that was risky, whether she was involved or not."

"She's the one who showed up on my doorstep asking to borrow the book," I said. "I know she's dangerous. The only vampire I've met who wasn't a manipulator is Dominic and he wound up dead. Oh, and the guy sleeping in the basement, but he doesn't count."

"I forgot about him," said Xavier. "Believe it or not, I've met plenty of amiable vampires."

"Guess I haven't been part of the paranormal world that long," I said. "Sometimes it feels like I have, but I haven't."

"It does to me," said Xavier. "It feels like you've been here forever."

My heart seized. Why did he have to say things like that? Maybe it was for the best that he stuck around town, because his absence had somehow only amplified my attraction to him, whatever the Grim Reaper did to keep the two of us apart.

"I guess I've run into more trouble than most people encounter in a lifetime," I said. "And now we're about to go nosing around Mr Blake's room to see if he left any clues behind that that relic hunter didn't find."

"Do you want to talk to him?" he asked.

"The only other people we can talk to who aren't being questioned by police are Mrs Peterson and the vampires," I said. "Not sure I want to try my luck with Evangeline again."

"I think we should speak to Mr Dreyer first, just to cover all the bases," he said. "Perhaps the murderer *is* a rogue, though, which means Evangeline's on our side, whether she knows or not."

"Then why would she tell me about Mrs Peterson and not about potential rogue vampires?" I said. "That makes no sense. By everything I've heard, Mr Spencer's ex-wife seems the *least* likely to have bumped off the two hunters. She didn't even know Mr Blake that well, and she wasn't involved in her ex-husband's lifestyle."

"Perhaps not, but we should tell her about Mr Blake's death and find out if there's anything else she knew about his friendship with her ex-husband," he said.

I nodded. "All right. We'll speak to her first, since her shop is closer than the hotel. Then we'll go to see Mr Dreyer and see what else he's hiding."

———

Once again, we made our way to Mrs Peterson's shop. When we entered, she looked up at us with a mildly irritated expression on her face. "You again?"

"Hey," I said to her. "I don't know if you heard—but Mr Blake is dead."

"We were on our way to talk to him when they found

his body," Xavier explained. "He appeared to have jumped, or been pushed, out of his third-floor hotel bedroom window."

"He's dead? Really?" Her brows rose. "Do the police think it wasn't an accident?"

"Not sure yet," I said, "but another guest was spotted sneaking around his room earlier. Do you know Mr Dreyer?"

She gave me a blank look. "Should I?"

"He's some kind of relic collector, visiting town. I would have thought he might be interested in some of your wares."

"Oh, *him*," she said. "He tried to buy some of my best relics and offered me a pittance for them, as though I don't know my own trade. Then I caught him trying to slip one of those knives into his pocket. I'd keep an eye on those books of yours."

"He hasn't come to the library," I said. "Did he look like the type of person who'd go to extreme lengths to get his hands on rare objects?"

Extreme lengths... like committing murder, for instance?

"I can see it, but don't quote me on that," she said. "As for the vampire hunters, I never meant to get involved with those people to begin with. I haven't seen this Mr Blake since his arrival in town."

She sounded sincere enough, even without Blair's ability to confirm her words.

"So aside from Mr Dreyer, the only other possible suspect is someone who they both made an enemy of," I said. "Considering they were vampire hunters, and a vampire was spotted outside the hotel—"

"Evangeline's the one you need to speak to, not me," she said. "I've washed my hands of any connection with them *and* the vampires they used to hunt."

"We did talk to her," I said. "That is—before Mr Blake died. I've no doubt she'd know if there were any rogues in town, but she's not exactly looking out for my family's safety. And considering the book is now in my family's possession…"

"I'm afraid Mr Bennet would know more about cursed books than I would," she said. "I prefer to deal with ancient things that can't speak or communicate."

Or with fangs, I'd bet. "Thanks for talking to us anyway."

I doubted the book would talk to a stranger when it wouldn't even communicate with my family. Maybe the curse-breaker would know how to crack it open, but I wasn't sure the book was cursed. Just under a sentience spell.

As for Mr Dreyer? His unscrupulous antics didn't paint him in a favourable light, but snooping around Mr Blake's room wasn't the same as murdering someone. We needed more proof before we asked the police to question him again.

"Do you think he did it? Mr Dreyer?"

Xavier was silent for a long moment. "I think it was most likely a vampire. But it's worth having a closer look to see if any other relics may have fallen into his hands?"

I arched a brow. "You want to break into *his* room?"

"My Reaper powers will ensure he doesn't see me," he said. "What my boss doesn't know won't hurt him."

"Are you sure you should be pushing your luck?" I said.

"I mean, there might still be a rogue vampire hanging around looking for trouble."

The instant the words left my mouth, I realised how ridiculous I sounded. I mean, Xavier was immortal, and even the living dead couldn't harm him.

His mouth curled up at the side. "Are you worried about me?"

"Nope." He didn't need to have Blair's lie-sensing ability to know that for a lie. "I just forgot you were superhuman for a second there. Anyway, there *is* a vampire around."

"I doubt he'll be near the hotel," he said. "That Mr Dreyer strikes me as unscrupulous at best, but if a rogue vampire is the killer, they'd have no reason to stick around now the two hunters are dead."

"Unless that's not all they came here for." The image of the book appeared in my mind's eye. "Evangeline would know. She must do. But whether she's involved or not, I wouldn't trust her to warn my family of the danger. Not without forcing us to strike a deal with her, at any rate."

"There's one person Evangeline is afraid of," he said. "My boss."

Hmm. "Is she really? I mean, he can't reap *her* soul."

"I've never been clear on that one, to tell you the truth," he said. "If I tell him I suspect she might be connected to the case and to arrange a meeting with her, then he'll do so. And she'll have to accept."

My throat closed up even thinking about what she'd say if she suspected I'd set the Grim Reaper on her. "Let's put that in the 'last resort' category. My aunts are trying to wrangle information from Edwin on whether or not any of the guests knew the secret to unlocking the book.

If we get proof from the book itself, we won't need to involve your boss. Hopefully, Aunt Adelaide and Estelle will be back in the library by now."

"Sure," said Xavier. "I'll have to tell my boss about Mr Blake, but he doesn't insert himself in human affairs unless there's a threat to our own kind. I'll drop by the relic hunter's room tonight and see if I can find anything. Don't worry about me, Rory—I promise I'll be fine."

He took my hand and pulled me into a hug. For a heart-stopping instant, I thought he was going to kiss me, but he released me, leaving my hands tingling.

I am so screwed.

When I got back to the library, it was to find that Aunt Adelaide and Estelle still weren't back yet. Instead, Cass occupied the front desk, looking bored. "You're back. Is nobody going to come and take over from me?"

"It doesn't look like we've had many visitors," I said. "Did you tell Aunt Candace she might need a password to get into the book?"

"Yes," said Cass. "Now she's locked up in that room yelling nonsense words at the book. I put *three* sound-proof spells on the door, and nobody's come here to thank me for it."

"Thank you," I said. "Better?"

"I've had bloody enough of that book," said Cass through clenched teeth. "It's scaring off our customers, it's terrifying my pets, and now my mum and sister are off dealing with the police instead of this stack of returns." She indicated a towering pile of books that had popped up beside the desk.

"Isn't Sylvester around?" I asked.

"He got it into his head that he needed to help out with

the passwords. So did that familiar of yours." She glared at the book pile. "This has gone on for way too long. We need to lock that book away or throw it out."

Now I knew where she was coming from. For Cass, anger was a defence mechanism, and given her concern over her animals, it was no wonder she was being snappier than usual with everyone today.

"We owned the book to begin with, though." I moved around the desk to where the logbook lay. "If more than one book is activated via a password, isn't there a list?"

"There is," she said. "I can't find it. I assume Aunt Candace borrowed the damned thing for a book and then lost it. I found the list of passwords for the doors that require special access, but not the ones for actual books."

"Hmm." I pulled out my Biblio-Witch Inventory. One of the prominent words in there was *find.* It was intended so that I'd be able to find my way out if I ever got lost, but it had multiple uses.

"It won't work if you don't know what the password list looks like," Cass said. "If you want to make yourself useful, return some of those books, since nobody else is going to bother to help me."

———

Cass and I had almost finished with the mountain of returns by the time Estelle returned, and Aunt Adelaide didn't get back until dinner was already in the oven. We were loading our plates when she walked in, looking frazzled.

"Finally," Aunt Candace said, taking a huge bite of

mashed potato. "I was starting to think you and Edwin had hooked up."

Estelle choked on a sip of juice. "Really, Aunt Candace."

"I was delayed at the police station," said Aunt Adelaide, levitating her plate onto the table. "Edwin and his people insisted on me telling them everything about the book, which led to me having to explain all our confidentiality policies."

"We had better luck back here," Cass said. "We found out the book is activated with a password, but *someone* lost the list."

Aunt Adelaide sat down and turned to her sister. "What did you do with the paper? Borrowed it for a book?"

Aunt Candace took a long time chewing her mouthful. "I won't say I *didn't*, but I thought I put it back."

Aunt Adelaide picked up her fork. "Well, Edwin's being unhelpful. Supposedly, everything is in the police's hands now and we're not to touch the case, unless we're prepared to hand over the book."

I looked up. "We were wondering if either victim had a personal record of how to open the book. Mr Spencer must have known, right?"

"If he did, the police don't have it," said Aunt Adelaide. "According to Edwin, both men were both minimalist travellers and carried nothing but clothes."

"That can't be right," I said. "If they were here to hunt down a vampire, wouldn't they have brought... I don't know, weapons?"

"Edwin didn't say," said Estelle. "I wondered the same. Perhaps the police confiscated them, but it's not in their interests to spread rumours that rogue vampire hunters are in town. They aren't well thought-of generally, and everyone knows not to cross Evangeline."

"True, but you'd think they'd have *something*. Like stakes or garlic…"

Cass snorted. "Garlic?"

"It's a normal world legend," I said. "They say vampires are allergic to garlic. Then again, the legends also say they burst into flames in sunlight, which isn't true either."

"Or sparkle," said Aunt Candace. "In my books, some of them turn into spiders. Keeps things interesting."

Aunt Adelaide pressed her lips together. "Perhaps the police need to conduct a more thorough search of their rooms."

Yeah. Or Xavier. I wished I could go with him, but I didn't have that handy Reaper ability to walk through walls when it suited me.

"Maybe," I said. "But why are they so interested in the book? Do they think there's a connection after all?"

"Edwin isn't ruling anything out," she said. "He knows the two ex-hunters were acquainted with one another, but their research is still a step behind ours. He also spoke with the Reaper earlier."

"Yes, the Reaper is back in town," said Aunt Candace, her eyes gleaming. "What an interesting turn of events."

I felt my face heat up as Cass made a derisive noise. "For some of us, maybe."

"I'm not surprised," said Aunt Adelaide. "The Reaper has nobody else to take his place, so I expected they'd return eventually."

Then why would the Grim Reaper have left that note, except to warn me off? If so, I was pushing my luck by working with Xavier again, but even if I removed my personal feelings from the equation, he'd been present for both murders and knew as much as I did.

And if the vampires *were* involved, I could at least count on them fearing the Reaper.

11

Luck wasn't with us. Xavier showed up the following day with the news that Mr Dreyer had left town in the early hours of the morning.

"I did look around his room during the night, but I had to leave when he woke up," he explained. "I didn't see any evidence that he knew about the book, nor how to open it. We'll either need to ask Frederick if we can have another look around his room, or speak to Edwin about our concerns and see if we can persuade him to send someone after him."

"Aunt Adelaide already did," I said. "Supposedly, both Mr Blake and Mr Spencer were minimalist travellers who only brought clothes on their vampire-slaying mission."

His brows shot up. "I didn't find any weapons or anything either. Perhaps I can convince Frederick to let me take a look in both empty rooms."

"Depends if he knows two of his guests were ex-vampire hunters or not." Aunt Adelaide had implied

Edwin hadn't wanted word to spread, but it was unlikely Evangeline didn't know by this point.

Inside the hotel, we found Frederick sitting behind the reception desk, his eyes red-rimmed with tiredness and even his lopsided grey hat dull and drooping.

"What is it this time, Reaper?" he said. "Please tell me nobody else is dead."

"No, but I wanted to ask you about Mr Dreyer," said Xavier. "Have the police questioned him again?"

"He's gone," said Frederick. "He checked out of the hotel this morning."

"I'm sorry to hear that," said Xavier, with perfectly feigned surprise. "I heard he was trespassing in one of the victims' rooms. I don't know if you've heard the latest from the police—"

"There was no evidence to back up that claim besides eyewitness accounts, and the police didn't think that enough to take him into custody," he said. "I have other guests scheduled to stay in that room, and they'll be arriving later today."

"Understandable," said Xavier. "You should know, though… word has made it to my boss that the two who died were involved in illicit activities."

Frederick's whole demeanour changed. "The Grim Reaper? *He's* not with you, is he?"

"No, but I feel it's best to assuage his doubts. May I have a look around the empty room?"

His shoulders slumped. "Look, this has been bad enough for business as it is, and I do not think any of my guests were involved in the two tragic deaths. If the Grim Reaper shows up on my doorstep next, the rest of the guests will flee in terror and I might as well close up the hotel for good."

"He won't come here," Xavier said, his tone soothing. "But if Mr Dreyer's behaviour was suspicious, wouldn't it be better to clear things up now? I won't leave a trace."

"I suppose." He heaved a sigh, then fetched a key from behind the counter and handed it to Xavier. "Be quick, Reaper."

We headed upstairs, Xavier in the lead. "Mr Dreyer was staying on the first floor… same as Mr Spencer."

"And Mr Blake was up on the third floor," I added. "Your boss isn't coming, is he?"

"No." He spoke in a low voice. "I don't like using his name to pressure others, but it sounds like Edwin is missing some crucial pieces of evidence."

Searching Mr Dreyer's room didn't take long. The suite was pristine and ready for the next guests, and if the relic collector had taken anything, he'd left no traces behind. Xavier and I opened all the drawers in the room and checked under the bed, in the wardrobe, even behind the curtains. None of them held any traces of the room's last inhabitant.

"And Mr Spencer's room?" I said. "I know if there was anything in there, it's more likely to have been removed, but he can't have planned to hunt down vampires with no weapons."

"Agreed." He led the way down the corridor. "As far as I know, no new guests have moved into his room yet."

Mr Spencer's room took even less time to search. Whoever had cleaned it had been thorough in removing every sign of habitation, and if any subtle signs remained, Xavier would be more likely to see them, not me.

"Anything?" I asked him.

He shook his head. "Let's check Mr Blake's room, then we'll leave."

One room to go. We climbed to the third floor to look for the room where Mr Blake had met his untimely end.

Xavier tried the door. "Locked."

"Why not get the key for that one?"

He answered by walking *at* the door, as though it wasn't there, and vanished through its wooden surface. Then the door opened from the inside and Xavier welcomed me in with a smile.

"You're unbelievable, you are." I didn't move. "Also, you know I can't tread lightly without leaving a trace like a Reaper, don't you?"

"You won't contaminate the crime scene." He beckoned me into the room, and I slipped behind the door, resigned. The Reaper was a bad influence on me, that was for sure.

The window Mr Blake had fallen out of was closed now, sealed shut. I looked from the window to the door, mentally calculating the distance. Unless he'd been standing right next to the window when he'd died, the person who'd pushed him must have shoved him all the way across the room by force. A human might have subdued Mr Blake first, but I couldn't picture an ex-vampire hunter being easy to sneak up on. Which left one option remaining.

Vampire.

The small hairs stood up on my arms. How could the police arrest a rogue vampire who nobody had seen? Except for Mr Dreyer's midnight sighting, and it didn't sound like anyone had taken his word for it, let alone pieced together an accurate description. No... it was Evangeline we needed to consult, assuming one of her own people wasn't responsible.

Xavier halted in the room's centre, turning on the spot. "The killer didn't force the door. That much we know."

"There aren't any signs of a fight either." Though given the crimson swirling patterns on the carpet, bloodstains would be easy to hide.

Xavier shook his head. "I may have to bring up my boss in front of Edwin next."

Or Evangeline.

Resigned, I headed downstairs with Xavier at my side. How had the killer left no traces? For that matter, how could two vampire hunters have carried nothing that so much as hinted at their choice of profession?

Unless someone else had removed them. Someone who moved faster than a human did.

As we reached the ground floor, my foot kicked a piece of the carpet loose at the foot of the stairs. Frowning, I halted. The carpet was slightly torn up the side, on the area where Mr Spencer had fallen. And underneath the raised section—

"What are you doing?" asked Xavier.

I crouched down at the foot of the stairs where Mr Spencer's body had lain. "Do you see that?"

Xavier crouched beside me and lifted a corner of the carpet. A red stain darkened the wall beneath it. My heart lurched. "That... I don't think it's paint."

Frederick trod towards us. "What is it?"

"That's where Mr Spencer fell." I pointed. "But it's not his blood, I don't think."

The hotel owner went very pale at the sight of the blood staining the wall.

"I'll call the police," he said, his voice tremulous. "You two… you should leave."

We left the hotel. There wasn't much else to do. It wasn't until we reached the walkway to the beach that Xavier held up a thread, soaked in blood. He must have used his swift Reaper speed to yank out part of the carpet while Frederick wasn't looking.

"Good job," I said. "Estelle knows a spell which can track the owner of someone's blood. Want me to give it to her?"

"Sure," he said. "Frederick means well, but I think one of us should stick around here to make sure the police have the right impression."

"Meaning you." Only witches could use magic to identify someone using their blood, so I'd have to ask one of my family members. "I can't think whose blood it might be, though. Mr Spencer didn't have any visible injuries. As for Mr Blake, he was nowhere near the stairs when he fell out of the window."

"It's not a fresh stain." He examined the thread. "But it's not that old either, I don't think. A week at most."

A week. He'd know, since he spent enough time around dead bodies, so I'd have to take his word for it.

"I'll see what Estelle says." I gingerly took the thread from him, suppressing a shudder. "Be careful."

"You, too."

I hurried through the town square, careful to hide the bloody thread in my hand to avoid anyone asking awkward questions. Despite my jangling nerves, I reached the library without incident and caught up to Estelle at the front desk.

"Estelle," I said. "You know that spell you used to check whose blood was on that coat a while ago? I need to know how to use it."

"What?" She blinked at the sight of the blood-soaked thread of fabric. "Rory, what is that?"

"We found blood under the carpet on the stairs where Mr Spencer died," I explained. "The police are on their way to the scene, but I wanted to see if we could figure out whose blood it is. I'm not convinced it belonged to Mr Spencer."

Estelle took the thread from me in one hand and drew her wand with the other. "I can teach you, but it's quite a bit beyond a beginner's level spell."

With her wand hand, she made a complex gesture. The thread glowed a little, and she gasped aloud.

"What is it?"

Estelle lowered a trembling hand. "The blood isn't human blood. It belongs to a vampire."

My mouth dropped open. "Which vampire?"

"I don't know," she said. "But the blood wouldn't be glowing like that if it belonged to a human."

My heart began to beat faster. "Did Mr Spencer or Mr Blake kill a vampire while they were staying here?"

What had they done with the body, then? And what weapons had they used? *We're missing something big here.*

"I couldn't say," she said. "If they killed a vampire, I would have thought they'd have used a stake, which turns vampires to ash and leaves no traces behind, nor any blood."

"Dominic didn't turn to ash when he died," I said,

thinking of how I'd run into his body lying in the street. "Besides, we found no weapons. Even if the vampire was injured and not dead, how'd they dispose of the body without being noticed? Unless... unless the vampire survived and ran, then came back to kill them later?"

"Ask the vampires," said Estelle. "In fact... no. Don't ask the vampires. That's a really bad idea."

"If we start looking up 'how to get rid of a vampire's body', the police will add us to a watchlist," I said.

"Nah, Aunt Candace looks stuff like that up frequently and she's never been arrested," said Estelle. "Except for that one time, I mean."

"She dated a vampire. Might she know?"

"Would she really have asked the guy she was dating how she'd hide his dead body?" Estelle pursed her lips. "On second thoughts, that *is* exactly the kind of question she'd ask. Let's find her."

If there was one thing you could count on, it was Aunt Candace's ability to turn everything into a research opportunity. Estelle disposed of the bloody thread and we made our way to the classroom at the back of the ground floor which had become Aunt Candace's second home over the last few days.

I rapped on the door. "Aunt Candace?"

"She won't hear us if the soundproofing spell is in effect." Estelle tapped a word in her Biblio-Witch Inventory and the door sprang open.

"What is it this time?" Aunt Candace looked up from the book. "I can't find the password, and that's not for lack of trying. I've used hundreds of languages, and that crow of yours has lost his voice."

Jet, who sat on the table, gave a feeble croak.

"I'll get him out of here," I said, holding out a hand for my familiar to hop onto. "That's not what we wanted to ask. Hypothetically, how would one go about getting rid of a vampire's body?"

Her gaze sharpened in an instant. "Hypothetically? Well, well… it's always the quiet ones, isn't it?"

"I haven't killed anyone!" I said. "We think a vampire was killed at the hotel, but a body hasn't been found. Just blood. Vampire blood."

"At the scene where Mr Spencer died," Estelle added. "I tested it myself and the blood didn't belong to a human. No doubt the police will come to the same conclusion, but this whole situation has me stumped. Who did the blood belong to?"

"You're asking me?" said Aunt Candace. "I can't even remember the password for this blasted book."

The book made a hissing noise. "I'm tired of listening to your whining, too."

She ignored the book. "Perhaps it was old blood from a past murder. Or the body is buried under the floorboards."

"I'm fairly sure Frederick would have noticed," I said. "The hotel is right by the beach, so throwing it into the ocean would be the quickest way to get rid of a body… assuming nobody caught them at it."

"If it didn't wash back onto the shore again," added Estelle. "Like that poor academy kid."

"He wasn't a vampire, though," I reminded her. "He was faking. I guess the vampire the blood belonged to might have been injured and escaped, but that's just guesswork. I mean, nobody saw them, that we know of."

The sound of a door opening came from within the lobby.

Estelle glanced over her shoulder. "Someone's at the front desk."

"Close the door behind you," said Aunt Candace. "And do tell me if you find out whose blood it is. I want to put *that* in my next mystery book."

"Honestly." I closed the door and Estelle redid the soundproofing spell. "At least she's staying out of trouble."

I found Xavier standing beside the front desk. "Hey, Rory."

"Did you speak to Edwin?" I asked. "That was fast."

"I caught him on his way to the crime scene," he said. "Both he and Frederick insist they have no idea whose blood was on the stairs."

I swallowed hard. "We found out the blood's owner was a vampire, but Estelle's spell couldn't pin down whose it was."

"A *vampire?*" His eyes widened. "One of them killed a vampire?"

"Or injured them," said Estelle. "Perhaps Mr Spencer did, but the vampire got behind him and pushed him downstairs. Then the vampire fled the crime scene. You know how fast they move. It's not implausible, right?"

"True, but I think I'd have noticed if he'd been fighting a vampire when he spoke to me on the phone," I said. "And he would have been carrying a weapon if he'd expected an attack. The police didn't find any on him, let alone in his room."

"I prompted Edwin to take another look into their history as vampire hunters," said Xavier. "He agrees that the evidence supports the fact that the two of them weren't as retired as it appeared. Perhaps that's what they wanted to lead the vampires to believe."

"Except they came here with no weapons, or other vampire-hunting gear." I glanced over my shoulder in the direction of the Reading Corner. "Do the police think they might have wanted to use the book as bait? Is that why they're so interested in it?"

"Maybe." Xavier's forehead creased. "Edwin told me he'll take into consideration that Mr Dreyer may have seen a vampire near the hotel, but since he didn't report the incident to the police, it's not enough to merit alerting the vampires."

"Evangeline knows," said Estelle. "There's no way she doesn't."

"I know," I said. "Most of the *town* knows about the screaming book, so it's not exactly a low-key method of baiting the vampires without drawing anyone else's attention. Why did Mr Spencer foist it on us to begin with if he didn't want to make us into targets?"

"Maybe he knew he was being chased," said Xavier. "And he gave you the book so that you'd be able to track his killer if he died."

"He didn't look like he expected to die when we first met." I frowned. "He just seemed desperate to have that book off his hands. As soon as he handed it over, he scarpered. I don't understand why he left us to take the fall. We didn't know him."

"No, we didn't," said Estelle. "What happened to the relic hunter, then?"

"He's gone," I said. "He left town this morning. We looked around his room, but he left no traces behind either."

"I searched Mr Blake's and Mr Spencer's rooms, too," added Xavier. "Until Rory stumbled upon the blood on the stairs, we found nothing. It seems the two vampire hunters came to town with no weapons nor any means of body disposal."

"Nor any instructions on how to open the book," I added.

"Did you ever find out when Mr Spencer checked it out?" asked Xavier. "Because even if he did know how to open it, it strikes me as impractical to carry a book around for months or years with no way to stop it from screaming."

"Nope." Estelle rubbed her forehead. "The problem is, none of us can remember who it was who loaned him the book to begin with. You know how many people we deal with on an annual basis from within the town, let alone outside it. You need a licence to get some of the more dangerous books and I assume he had one, but we still haven't found the record."

"Or the password list," I said. "Which Aunt Candace lost somewhere."

"All we know is that the return date was New Year's Day, just after midnight," said Estelle. "The book was set to start screaming if it was returned late, so perhaps Mr Spencer decided to turn his trip into a vampire-hunting mission. It might not have been planned at all."

"And Mr Blake just happened to show up?" Planning a vampire-hunting mission around an unreliable book that screamed constantly seemed unlikely, too. "In the same town Mr Spencer's ex-wife lives in, too?"

"You think she's involved?" asked Xavier.

"Your guess is as good as mine," I said. "She's the only

non-vampire suspect still around now Mr Dreyer is gone."

"Mr Dreyer…" Estelle paused. "You know, I did get his phone number when I was researching. I can see if he's still reachable."

"Do you think he'll answer, though?" I said. "If he was up to anything dodgy, he won't want to be followed."

Xavier's expression turned thoughtful. "There is *one* way to track him, but it would involve using my Reaper powers."

"Your…" I trailed off. "You can find people. Right?"

"A Reaper can track anyone without being near them," he said. "If he's in the general area, I can convince him to come back and make a statement to the police. Then there'll be more than our word as proof of the vampires' involvement. Evangeline will have to get involved publicly."

"Can the Grim Reaper track people in the same manner?" I asked. "So he *would* know if a rogue vampire was in town?"

"Not a vampire," he said. "They aren't trackable the same way humans are. Look, this is… classified. But I can certainly find Mr Dreyer."

"So can a tracking spell, and they don't carry scythes," I said. "You won't tell your boss?"

"I won't," he said. "Just give me a few minutes, okay? I'll be back before you know it."

"Okay, but—be careful."

As the door closed behind him, Sylvester flew down to land on the desk. "Trouble in paradise?"

"I thought you'd still be arguing with the book," I commented. "Got bored, did you?"

"If that thing is password-activated, I'm a cactus," said the owl.

Estelle turned to the owl. "Aunt Candace is still trying out passwords. You mean she's wasting her time?"

"It keeps her out of my hair," said Sylvester.

"You don't have hair," I said. "As you told me yourself. Anyway, you're the one who's supposed to be in charge of late returns. How come you didn't know about this one?"

"Because unlike some people, I take New Year's Eve off," he said self-importantly.

"Really." I rolled my eyes. "You should know, we're pretty certain the book was planted here as bait to lure in rogue vampires, but the two people who were hunting them managed to get themselves killed."

"Bait!" He gave a loud squawk, his wings extending so suddenly one of them hit me in the face. The other knocked the logbook off the table.

"Ow." I stepped back out of reach of his talons. "Yes, bait. Have you not been paying any attention?"

"Candace lost the password sheet, did she?" He landed back on the desk, his head rotating to face me. "I knew I should have taken that book apart."

"What are you talking about?" said Estelle. "Look—honestly. You've made me lose my page."

She scooped up the logbook and then held it out of reach as Sylvester gave it a jab with his beak. "There's no record in there."

"Stop that," Estelle said. "What's the matter with you?"

The owl spread his wings wide and launched into flight, saying over his shoulder, "I'm going to save Candace's skin. Again."

Estelle put the logbook down. "That bird. I only got

halfway through the long-term loans and now I've lost my page."

"He said there's no record," I said slowly. "You don't think it's odd that *none* of us can get the book open? I mean, Aunt Adelaide managed to open a book the other week where you have to answer a riddle to open each chapter. You'd think we'd have figured out how to stop the screaming by now."

The logbook slipped from her hands onto the front desk. "What are you saying?"

"I'm saying the book might not even have been ours in the first place."

Estelle shook her head. "No… it is ours. It's definitely on our list."

"But does the list say whether it was taken out or not?" I asked.

Estelle flipped open the logbook and began frantically turning pages. "I was searching for Mr Spencer's name—but if he *didn't* check it out—"

I fidgeted, wondering when Xavier would come back, as she skimmed the logbook until she came to a halt. "The book is still out there. That one… that one's a fake."

"What?" I stared at her. "How? It's a sentience spell, right?"

"That doesn't make it one of ours." Estelle dropped the logbook on the desk. "I'll have to break the news to Aunt Candace, if Sylvester hasn't already."

"I think he has," I said. "But your mum needs to know, too. I'll wait for Xavier—I thought he was going to take a minute or two."

Had something gone wrong? *He can't be in danger. He's the Reaper.*

While Estelle hurried through the stacks in search of her mother, I pushed open the doors and peered outside, cursing the Grim Reaper for refusing to let Xavier carry a mobile phone so I could check what was taking him so long.

A chill brushed against my neck. As though my thoughts had conjured him up, the Grim Reaper appeared in the doorway before me, his scythe in his hands.

12

Darkness flooded the library, so dark it turned the shelves to hunched shadows and masked every source of light. Whenever I set eyes on the Grim Reaper, I forgot how to speak, how to think. He looked at me, and the breath froze in my lungs. I stumbled backwards, catching my balance on the front desk.

"Where," he said, "is my apprentice?"

My tongue unstuck itself from the roof of my mouth. "He's on the tail of someone we suspect might be a murderer."

"Someone *you* suspect?"

I swallowed against my dry throat. "The suspect left town but is still in the area." I was starting to think he *wasn't* a suspect at all, but misleading the Grim Reaper was easier than admitting I'd sent his apprentice away for no reason. "The two people who were murdered at the hotel this week were vampire hunters. Mr Dreyer was the only witness who might have seen a rogue vampire in town."

"Vampires," he said. "Which vampire?"

"I don't know yet." I took a deep breath. "We have reason to believe a certain group of individuals are after one of the library's books. We know the two dead men were vampire hunters who used the book to lure their prey to town, but their plan went wrong."

I decided not to mention the book was a fake. I doubted the Grim Reaper would be impressed to know it had fooled all of us, and besides, Xavier really ought to have made it back by now.

"And why not leave it up to Evangeline?" he said. "She's the leader of the town's vampires and a more logical choice of confidant."

"Because she…" I hesitated. "She wants the book herself. And I don't trust her."

"Is that so?"

"Yes," I said, my voice growing steadier as my lies merged with the truth. "The book was planted in the library to turn my family into targets. Given her mind-reading skills, it wouldn't have been hard for Evangeline to find that information, yet she decided not to tell us we might be at risk."

"You're not naturally trusting," he mused. "I thought, given your interest in my apprentice, that you were naive as many humans are. But I seem to be mistaken."

My insides shrivelled up at the implication that he knew my feelings for Xavier, though it wouldn't be hard for him to figure it out by now. Despite my mortification and fear, I couldn't help wondering who had the Grim Reaper been, before he'd turned into this cold, terrifying being. I couldn't imagine him as human, but if he was really immortal, he wouldn't need an apprentice like

Xavier. That was a topic to ask Xavier himself about, though, not his boss.

"However, you're not telling me everything," he added. "Why would they target you, an unremarkable witch who grew up ignorant of the magical world? I don't think you're being entirely truthful with me, Aurora."

I have to tell him. It wasn't like *he* could use the journal, considering his total lack of interest in anything living. If vampires counted as living. If it came to it, he might even be able to help me deal with them.

"That's not all." I swallowed my fear. "I have a journal that used to belong to my dad. A group of vampires were already interested in obtaining the journal before I even moved to the library, including Mortimer Vale. He's in jail because he tried to steal it from me and two of his friends are still out there somewhere, so it's not unreasonable to assume the same group of people might be connected to the rogue vampires who killed two people at the hotel."

"And does my apprentice know all this?"

"Yes." I buried my freezing hands in my pockets. "So does my family."

"Irritating," he muttered. "If my apprentice became their target… this won't do. Fine. I will send you after him to find this suspect. I do hope that you don't disappoint me."

He stepped towards me, and I froze, my eyes caught on his scythe. *This is it. He's going to reap my soul this time, and I can't stop him—*

I squeezed my eyes shut, and a roaring wind blasted into me. When I opened my eyes, the library had disappeared, replaced by a long, curving road. A blond figure not ten feet away walked alongside a row of cottages painted in pastel shades. Despite my chattering teeth, my heart lifted at the sight of Xavier. *He's okay.*

The darkness receded, and the Grim Reaper was gone, as though he'd never been there to begin with.

Xavier started when he spotted me. "Rory? How'd you get here?"

"Your boss gave me a lift," I said, and his jaw dropped. "Believe it or not, he actually takes the vampire threat seriously, so I'm here to help you with your interrogation."

"I'm hoping it won't turn into an interrogation, but I'm glad to have you with me," he said. "I've never seen him use his power on a mortal before."

"He seemed to think you might be in danger just by knowing about my dad's journal," I added.

His brows rose. "You told him about that?"

"He didn't give me much of a choice," I admitted. "Besides, I had to tell him why I don't trust Evangeline despite the clear connection between this case and the vampires. He didn't indicate whether he believed me about *that* or not, but I'd rather be on his side than against him."

"Most people would agree," he said. "Mr Dreyer is somewhere in this village, which is a couple of miles from Ivory Beach."

"Can you sense his precise location or just the general area?" I asked.

"It depends if he's moving." He scanned the street. "He's close, but I reckon he knows he's being followed."

I walked alongside Xavier, and as we rounded a corner, I spotted Mr Dreyer's cloaked form walking out of a shop. The instant he spotted us, he stopped in his tracks.

"Hello," said Xavier. "We just want to ask you some questions."

The relic hunter turned and ran, but Xavier overtook him, blocking his path. I hurried to pen him in from the other side. I might not move as fast as Xavier did, but after the Grim Reaper himself had helped me get here, I couldn't afford to let Mr Dreyer run away again.

All the fight went out of him when he saw he was cornered. "What do you want? If it's my time to die, I'd be happy to pay you whatever I'm worth."

Xavier shook his head. "We're not here to take your life. We're here to ask you about the two people who were murdered at Ivory Beach's hotel this week. You were seen walking around Mr Blake's hotel room a few hours before his death. You haven't acted like an innocent man. Why were you there?"

"I was looking for relics," he said, his voice tremulous. "I didn't lie."

"But you wanted the book," I pushed. "Right? The one Mr Spencer returned to the library."

"The book was a fake," he blurted. "A creation of magic. I saw the instructions for creating it in Mr Blake's room when I searched. I don't doubt the original book is somewhere, but it's not with you in the library."

So it's true.

"Then is the real book still out there?" I said. "You're looking for it?"

"No," he said. "Certainly not. Two people are dead, and I don't want to join them, thank you very much. As soon as I found out the truth, I packed my bags and made preparations to leave."

"How *did* you find out?" I asked. "You didn't come to the library, and there was nothing in Mr Blake's room to suggest the book was a fake or otherwise."

He blinked. "The police must have taken the evidence away. I found notes all over his room, all about the spells he used and the people he hired to help create the fake book. It didn't look like an easy job."

"And did you put them back where you found them?" said Xavier.

"Of course I did." He raised his chin. "I'm done with this. It's not worth risking my life."

"But…" I frowned. "You knew they were vampire hunters, right? Didn't you see a vampire yourself, outside the hotel?"

"I'm starting to think I imagined it," he mumbled. "I was half asleep at the time, and you know… the guy looked like—"

He broke off, going even paler than he had when he'd seen us. Given the chill on the back of my neck and the way Xavier stiffened at my side, I could guess why.

Shadows spread behind me, heralding the arrival of the Grim Reaper. "That is not a vampire," he said. "You told me you were looking for a suspect."

My throat went dry. "I never said he was a vampire."

"You led me to believe my apprentice was in danger," he said, his voice low, dangerous.

Fear flooded me. "We haven't found the vampires who the two ex-hunters were trying to lure to town. The murderer is still at large."

"Yes, and what if there were souls in need of reaping

while my apprentice was busy helping you?" he said. "You divert his attention from his purpose and make him forget what he is."

"It's not like when he was under a spell," I said. "I wasn't stopping him from doing his job. He chose to come with me."

"You're a distraction and a liability," he said. "I told you not to contact him again."

"Someone is trying to play both of us. With the fear creeping up my throat, my voice was more of a squeak, but I pressed on. "Those vampire hunters planted a fake book in the library to lure vampire rogues to town, only for it to backfire and them to end up dead. Xavier became involved by default when he had to take their souls to the afterlife."

"And his involvement should have stopped there." The Grim Reaper moved closer to Mr Dreyer, who whimpered. "I will take this one to the police. My apprentice will come with me. And you, Aurora, will go back to the library."

For a heartbeat, I expected him to leave me here alone and force me to walk all the way back to Ivory Beach alone. Then shadows folded over my head, and I held my breath. An instant later, the darkness cleared, and I stood in the town square on the library's doorstep. Xavier was nowhere to be seen, and nor was the Grim Reaper.

I turned to face the library, my legs shaking. So much for catching the culprit. Despite his unscrupulous nature, Mr Dreyer had been an unlucky bystander, or so it seemed—and he'd be spilling his secrets to the police soon enough, one way or another.

I opened the library door with trembling hands and

slammed it closed behind me, my heart racing. How had I managed to land Xavier in hot water again? He'd end up taking the brunt of the blame, one way or another, and I could say goodbye to any tentative chances I might have had of rekindling our friendship.

"Rory!" Estelle looked alarmed. "What is it?"

"Oh, nothing," I breathed. "I just got chastised by the Grim Reaper for wasting his time, that's all."

"Ouch." She winced. "What went wrong? Didn't Xavier find Mr Dreyer?"

"He found him all right." I sucked in a breath. "But the Grim Reaper got mad at me for implying it was the vampires he was after. He claimed I was making it up on purpose to lure Xavier away from his job."

"I'm sorry, Rory," she said. "It's not good news here, either. Aunt Candace and Sylvester have been arguing over that wretched book for the last half-hour. As for my mum, she's been helping Cass re-settle all her pets. They got so freaked out by the book's screaming that they escaped and knocked a bunch of shelves all over the third floor. She has to deal with that before she comes to look at the book again."

"At least I'm not the only one having a bad day." I rubbed my eyes. "Whatever Aunt Candace thinks, it sounds like those two vampire hunters wanted to trick whoever they were hunting into coming here, so they made a fake copy of the book to lure them in. They left proof of the spell they used to create the fake book in Mr Blake's room, supposedly, but Xavier and I already searched and found nothing."

"Mr Dreyer told you that?" She blinked. "Is he with the police at the moment?"

"He is," I said. "The Grim Reaper took him there, in fact. But we need to find your mum. Cass, too. I think that book should be moved out of the library, fake or not. How is Sylvester handling it?"

"Not well. I think he's mad at Aunt Candace for not being quick enough on the uptake."

"Where's your mother?" I asked.

"Here." Aunt Adelaide descended the stairs. "Where have you been, Rory? Estelle said you found bloodstains belonging to a vampire at the hotel."

"We did, but we don't know whose," I explained. "Xavier and I went after Mr Dreyer to persuade him to come back to town and tell the police he saw a vampire from his window. He confirmed what we know—the book was a fake created using a spell. It was never ours, and he has no interest in the actual book now."

"It would explain why there are no recent records," Estelle added. "And the absence of the password sheet, too."

"I bet he moved it himself while he was here," I said. "He might even have done it while I was putting the book in its room. Sylvester took the night off, so he wasn't watching the ground floor like he normally is."

No wonder the owl was so miffed at the book for fooling all of us.

Aunt Adelaide rubbed her forehead. "It shouldn't be possible."

"Oh, it's perfectly *possible*," said Aunt Candace from behind us. "And clever. I should have known the book was a fake when I failed to unravel the security spells."

"You might have mentioned that." Aunt Adelaide's eye twitched. "You kept trying out passwords regardless?"

"Of course I did," said Aunt Candace. "Just because the book isn't one of ours doesn't mean I can't convince it to spill its secrets."

"It's a *fake*," said Estelle, emphasising the last word. "Cracking open the book won't get you anything. If I were you, I'd look for the password sheet instead."

"The relic hunter said he left town as soon as he found out it was a fake," I explained. "It sounded like the two vampire hunters thought they'd create a copy of this super-rare book order to lure over the vampires they were hunting. He said he found proof in their rooms, but Xavier and I didn't find a thing when we searched."

"Is that so?" said Aunt Candace. "How vexing."

She was taking this better than I'd thought. In fact, I could almost see the cogs turning in her mind, figuring out how best to turn this into a story.

"That's one way of putting it," said Aunt Adelaide. "If Mr Spencer wanted to put off all our customers by unleashing a screaming book on us, he certainly did a spectacular job."

"I don't think that was his intention," I said. "I doubt the two of them planned to end up dead, either."

"How careless of them," said Aunt Candace.

"Candace," said Aunt Adelaide, pinching the bridge of her nose. "Need I remind you that the fake book is still in our possession, and everyone in town knows it by now? This isn't over until the book is gone, and maybe not even then. The murderer has yet to be caught."

"Oh, don't be such a downer," said Aunt Candace. "There are no rogue vampires here. I suppose Evangeline and her people chased them off."

"It didn't sound that way," I said. "I think you should feed that book to one of Cass's pets, to be honest."

Estelle snorted. "Rory's right, you know."

"Edwin will want to see the book first," said Aunt Adelaide. "Is Xavier with him?"

My throat closed up. "No, but Mr Dreyer is, so Edwin will know soon enough."

"He's welcome to keep the book," said Aunt Candace. "Once I'm done with it, that is."

"Don't do anything rash." Aunt Adelaide looked up as Sylvester flew overhead, landing on the desk.

"The book's impervious to damage, too," he said. "I checked."

"Oh, good." Aunt Adelaide ran a hand through her hair. "We'll go and deal with that, then, shall we?"

She and Aunt Candace headed off, pursued by Sylvester. I hung back, unable to believe I'd overlooked the obvious.

Estelle glanced at me. "Did something else upset you, Rory? Is it Xavier?"

"Kind of." I looked down. "The Grim Reaper was convinced I tricked him into believing Xavier was in danger when he wasn't. He said I'm a distraction and a liability. Then he took him away, probably to put him under house arrest."

"Oh, Rory," she said. "You know that's not true. He's— well, the Grim Reaper. He's not even human."

"Neither is Xavier," I said. "A fact both of us keep forgetting."

"He's not the type to string you along, is he?" she said. "He must still think you have a chance of remaining friends, at least."

"We're talking about the guy who didn't even know his boss had left me a threatening note." I shook my head. "This time, he might do worse. To Xavier, even."

Yet I didn't know if I could cut him out of my life again. Not now.

"Give it time." She hugged me. "Want to go and watch a movie? We haven't done that for a while."

"Sounds good." I smiled.

Whatever happened, my family had my back. Now we knew the book for what it was, the truth would come out, one way or another.

13

This time, when Sylvester woke me up by hooting in my ear, I groaned and buried my head under the pillow. "Go away."

"That's not very nice," he said. "I thought you needed my help."

"I never said I did." I yawned. "I know, I know, I shouldn't have sent Xavier after Mr Dreyer, but if I hadn't, I'd still assume the book was real and not a fake."

"Are you quite finished?" The owl landed on the bed, his claws digging into the duvet. He was surprisingly heavy.

"You're standing on my arm," I protested. "What do you mean by offering me help? Are you inviting me for a free trip into the Forbidden Room?"

"Free? You're free to do whatever you like."

"Yes, I know that." I needed a bucket of coffee to wake up before finishing this conversation. "But you said I'm only allowed one question a day."

"I did. You haven't used today's yet."

I hadn't used yesterday's, either. There'd been little point, since Sylvester could only answer questions about what was already in the library. The fake book had never been ours, while the vampires hadn't set foot in here at all.

"I always ask the wrong questions." I buried my head in the pillow again.

"Yes, you do." Sylvester climbed up my arm and dug his claws in, making me wince. "So do most people, including your aunts."

"If this is supposed to be a pep talk, it's not working," I muttered into the pillow.

"I might add that you're the first member of the Hawthorn family in a long while who's come close to guessing what I am, or how I'm connected to the library."

"I suppose I did." I hadn't thought of it that way. Knowing Sylvester's secret hadn't made me any better at managing the owl's unpredictable nature, after all.

"Also," he added. "One of our books is rather overdue, and I *am* in charge of late fees, after all."

I lifted my head. "But it isn't our book."

"It's in the library, isn't it? That makes it ours."

"You're not going to stop until I get up, are you?" I rolled my eyes. "All right, I'll give the Forbidden Room a try."

The owl took flight and left the room. I, meanwhile, gathered my clothes and my wits. When I'd first discovered the Forbidden Room, I'd thought it contained the answers to any question I might want to ask. Since then, the room had proven as capricious as the owl himself, and the limit of one question per day had led me into trouble more than once. We already knew the truth about everything except the killer's identity and how the two vampire hunters had made the evidence of their deception disappear. The room wouldn't be able to help with either of those questions.

No… Sylvester wanted me to ask about the book, even though it didn't belong to the library. That was our speciality, and while the book itself had never been ours, perhaps the Forbidden Room would be able to shed some light on how to convince it to spill some secrets about its creators.

I thought over my options as I walked downstairs and crossed the lobby to the front desk, retrieving the Book of Questions from its shelf on the way. A plain black-covered book with a question mark on the cover, it didn't *look* like it contained information on every book in the library and a lot more besides.

Sylvester swooped down and landed on the front desk. "Your aunts have both tried and asked the wrong questions, so it's up to you."

"No pressure, then?" I opened the book. "I wish to enter the Forbidden Room."

At once, the floor disappeared beneath my feet, and I tumbled forward into emptiness. The next thing I knew, my feet touched the ground inside a room with black-painted walls, floor and ceiling.

I took in a deep breath. "How would one go about convincing a stubborn book to give up its information?"

———

Blair gaped at me. "You mean the book was a fake?"

"You've got it." I pushed my hair out of my eyes as the chill wind off the ocean sought out every gap in my cloak.

Since Blair and Nathan would be going home on Monday, I'd decided to take one last chance to enlist her help in unravelling the magic that had created the fake book.

And when I gave the book its final questioning, I needed the aid of someone who had the ability to tell truth from lie.

"Wow." She went silent for a moment as we turned our backs on the seafront and walked towards the town square. "That book always struck me as strange, but after everything I saw in the library during your tour, I figured you'd seen weirder."

"You're not wrong," I said. "In my defence, it fooled my entire family, too, and they've worked in the library for a lot longer than I have."

That was the only reason I hadn't given up in despair, aside from Sylvester's so-called pep talk. He might not want to admit it, but he was irked that the vampire hunters had got the best of *him* as well as the rest of us.

"So you're saying the real book is still out there, way overdue, and screaming at its owner?" said Blair.

"Possibly," I said. "Records go missing all the time. So do books. I mean, there's an entire corridor that just vanished upstairs. I reckon Mr Spencer and Mr Blake were counting on us not guessing until it was too late, but neither of them intended to get themselves killed before they could complete their plans."

"And Mr Dreyer?" she said. "Do you reckon he's going after the real book?"

"I doubt he is, but he's not the issue." I reached the library door and pushed it open. "I'm more concerned with the vampires. The book stopped talking to us yesterday, but I have an incentive now."

Armed with what I'd learned in the Forbidden Room, I led Blair to the classroom at the back of the ground floor. The door was locked, the soundproofing spell in place.

Here goes nothing.

I opened the door and approached the book lying on the desk. "We've come to talk to you again."

The book remained still.

"Playing dead, is it?" said Blair.

"It was never really alive, but it's been doing that ever since we found out it's a fake." I grabbed the book and flipped it upside-down. Then I gave it a shake.

The book broke into a screaming fit. "Put me down!"

"It's over," I said. "You don't belong to the library at all. Give me one good reason why I shouldn't take you apart."

As the screaming continued, I flipped the book over and pulled out my pen. Then I pressed the tip of the pen to the spine, as the Forbidden Room had instructed. The nib dug in. One more second and the whole spell would unravel.

The book stopped screaming. "I'm not here by choice."

"You don't have a choice, because you aren't alive." I dropped the book back on the desk. "Is it true that Mr Blake and Mr Spencer planted you in here? Who exactly were they trying to lure to Ivory Beach?"

"I don't know! I'm only a prop." The book flipped open, showing blank pages. "I didn't deceive you, witchling. I showed you I had blank pages from the start. You just chose to believe otherwise."

I jabbed it with the pen again. "I can unravel the spell keeping you intact in a heartbeat. What's your game?"

The book gave a whimper. "I'm just a sentience spell, nothing more. I was told to stall you until the plan was complete. I don't know what went wrong. I can't *see* outside of the library, you know."

"It's telling the truth," said Blair. "So you don't know the names of the rogue vampires?"

"No," said the book. "I told you, I'm just a prop. A wizard created me, and I've been passed around between owners ever since. They were careful not to share their names, and they kept me locked inside a box the whole time they owned me."

"Convenient," I said. "Can't you describe them, then?"

"Of course not. I don't have eyes." The book shrank away from the point of my pen. "Talk to the vampires if you want to know about rogues. I can't tell you any more than that."

Evangeline. I'd always thought she was several steps ahead of me, but if the rogues were still at large and she *didn't* know they were out there, then she had to be warned. The Grim Reaper, too.

"We're done here," I told the book. "If it were up to me, I'd take you apart, but that's not my decision to make."

"I'm lost," Blair said from behind me, as I closed the door. "The book was a decoy, but its owners weren't supposed to die. I get that much, but how do these rogue vampires fit into it?"

"Honestly, Mr Spencer is the one who confuses me the most," I admitted. "Why did he call the library? Because he got cold feet and decided to warn me?" And he'd died. Right in the middle of that conversation. I groaned and pressed my hands to my eyes. "What a week."

Blair cleared her throat. "It's not just the book stressing you out, is it? Do you want to talk about it?"

I lowered my hands. "Let's just say I made the Grim Reaper very mad."

Her eyes rounded. "You mean *the* Grim Reaper? That's a thing?"

"You didn't know?" Then she couldn't judge me. "I'm sort of dating his apprentice. Well, I was, but it all went wrong. I led the Grim Reaper to believe there were rogue vampires after me so I could take his apprentice with me to investigate, and he wasn't happy to find there weren't any. I only have Mr Dreyer's word for it, and he said he was half asleep when he saw a vampire from the window anyway."

"I'll see if Nathan remembers anything else any of the guests said," said Blair. "I have to go back to the hotel and pack, but let me know if you figure anything else out, okay?"

"Sure." I stepped back when something furred brushed my legs. Blair's cat followed after her, though I was sure I hadn't seen him come in. *That's familiars for you.* I hadn't seen Jet in a while, but he'd been avoiding the book, no doubt. At least we'd have it off our hands soon, if nothing else.

I paced back to the front desk. Because I wasn't looking where I was going, I didn't see the trapdoor until I fell into it. Tumbling headfirst into darkness, I landed face-down on a mattress, groaning.

"Ow!"

I groaned and sat up. That hadn't happened for a while. The trapdoor didn't seem to stay in one specific location on the ground floor, but Cass had made a habit of pranking me with it when I'd first come to the library.

The only thing the small room contained was a coffin,

in which a vampire slept. Pale and dark-haired, the vampire lay still enough to seem dead, yet still alive. I stared at him for an instant, my mind starting to connect the dots.

There were no rogues, no vampire hunters… and only one possible explanation.

I pulled out my Biblio-Witch Inventory and levitated myself out of the trapdoor, landing on the edge.

"Did you fall in there again?" said Cass. "I thought you were supposed to be hunting a vampire. How can you do that when you freak out every time you see one?"

"That's not why." I closed the trapdoor on the vampire. "I didn't think… but it's the only explanation that makes sense."

"*You're* not making sense," said Cass. "What's the problem? What did that damned book do now?"

I sucked in a breath. "I need to call Edwin."

And then? I'd need to have a chat with the Grim Reaper, and hope that this time, I didn't push him over the edge.

14

———

After I'd finished speaking to Edwin, I hung up the phone. Then I left the library and walked through the square, heading for the uphill slope leading towards the church where the vampires lived, and the nearby cemetery which was home to the local Reapers.

On the left-hand side of the road, shadowy gravestones loomed from the darkness, and a cold breeze drifted over the rusty iron gate. I opened it, holding my breath when it creaked, then slipped inside. The cemetery was shrouded in darkness even in daylight, and the sun didn't seem to touch it at all. Reapers didn't need to be able to see to do their jobs, but it didn't fit Xavier's personality one bit.

I edged through the darkness towards a building hunched at the back of the cemetery. I'd expected the Grim Reaper to live somewhere fancier, but the plain brick house was modest compared to the vampires' church. Dark curtains filled all the windows, making the place look even gloomier. I reached for the old-fashioned door knocker, which looked like it would make enough noise to wake the dead—hopefully not in a literal sense.

"There's no need," said a cold voice at my shoulder. "My apprentice won't hear you."

My insides turned to ice. I turned on the spot to face the figure who'd crept up behind me, a blot of darkness against the already shadowy cemetery.

"It's not him I'm here to see." My heart thumped too hard, too fast, but I managed not to bolt for it and jump over the fence. Instead, I looked the Grim Reaper in the eyes—or where his eyes should be, anyway.

"Then what is it you want from me, mortal?" said the Grim Reaper.

"I have a question," I said. "Did Mr Spencer's soul definitely pass on to the afterlife?"

"My apprentice took care of that, not me."

"And what happens if a soul is brought back?" I asked. "After the person turns into a vampire?"

"That rarely happens," said the Grim Reaper. "Most newly turned vampires fall into a coma after being bitten, and their souls remain in their bodies without passing on."

I'd talked to Evangeline herself about vampires' souls before, and she'd said that Reapers dealt with mortal souls and not immortal ones. But she'd been talking about vampires who'd *already* been immortal.

Mr Spencer hadn't been bitten and fallen into a coma. He'd died, or so it had seemed. But there was one more way to create a vampire—using the blood of another vampire to heal a fatal injury.

I might not know anything about vampires' souls, and

perhaps Xavier didn't either, but the Grim Reaper would know for sure. "And if no biting was involved?"

There was a long pause. Then…

"Bring me proof," he said. "Only then will I consider helping you. For now, my apprentice will be staying here."

I should have expected as much. Xavier wouldn't be coming with me. I was on my own.

So be it.

When I'd called the police earlier, Edwin had probably thought I was cracking up. He'd insisted the bodies of the two vampire hunters were in the same condition he would expect them to be, given how long had passed since the murders. Vampires, however, were cold no matter the temperature, didn't have heartbeats, and were also remarkably good at appearing to be dead when they weren't. Just look at the guy who'd been sleeping in the basement of the library for the last few decades.

With that in mind, all I needed now was a motive, but it wasn't hard to guess.

I left the graveyard. My breath fogged the air as I walked at a swift pace, out of the cemetery and back down the road. It took until I reached Mrs Peterson's shop for my insides to thaw out.

Mrs Peterson looked up at me as I walked through the antique shop. "You again?"

"When you said your husband and Mr Blake were rivals," I said breathlessly, "how deep did that run? Would they have deliberately tried to sabotage one another?"

"Sabotage?" she said. "Well, they couldn't do anything without making it into a contest. Same with the other hunters, when it came down to it. Is that what you mean?"

"Would they have hurt one another intentionally?" I asked.

She blinked. "Howard had a quick temper, certainly, and I found that the same was true of most of the people he associated with."

If the two ex-vampire hunters had gone to the trouble of creating a fake book to lure in the vampires, Mr Blake wouldn't have been happy that his friend had got cold feet and tried to warn me. He might, for instance, have acted irrationally and then regretted his hasty decision enough to attempt to undo it the only way he knew how.

As I stepped out of the shop, cold breath whispered on the back of my neck. Out of the corner of my eye, I saw movement, a swift figure stepping around me too fast for me to take in his features.

Then the world blurred before my eyes, flying past, far too quickly, and I closed my eyes against the oncoming darkness.

———

My eyes flickered open. I'd been aware of being carried, but I hadn't dared open my eyes until I lay on solid ground. Given the cold stone beneath me, I assumed I must be indoors, but the room was dark as pitch and cold enough for my breath to fog the air.

Where I was, though, I could only guess. Vampires could run for miles at a time, and for all I knew, they'd taken me to the other side of the country. Even if I'd kept my eyes open, I'd never have been able to take it all in.

I gingerly touched my face. Everything was still intact.

The vampire could have killed me at any time during our hair-raising flight, yet he'd chosen to spare my life.

Movement stirred in the darkness and a tall, hooded figure moved into view. "Why," Mr Spencer's voice said, "did your family have to ruin everything?"

I squinted at the shadowy figure, my teeth chattering in the cold. "If you didn't want my family involved, why'd you dump that book on us to begin with?"

Mr Spencer moved closer. His steps were silent now, more so than before, but he wore the same hooded cloak that hid his face as he had the last time I'd seen him. "It was a mistake. I tried to warn you, but *he* got there first. He knows I've spent half my life hunting vampires, but he turned me anyway. Now I'm as good as dead."

"You *faked* your death," I corrected. "You could have set the record straight at any time and my family would have got rid of the book."

"I had no choice but to hide." His voice grew louder, echoing off the walls. "If the local vampires find me, they'll have my head. It's not as easy to keep still and pretend to be dead as it looks, believe me."

I had very little sympathy. "Are you planning to kill me?"

"Kill you?" he said. "No. I only kill the dead. I would have left you alone if you hadn't kept interfering, but I can't have you blabbing my secrets to the vampires' leader."

I swallowed hard, looking around. In the darkness, I could make out the shadowy edges of a room, while an unpleasant coppery smell hung in the background. Blood. I'd bet Mr Spencer had brought his blood supplies here to his new hideout along with his other possessions before they'd fallen into the police's hands.

"You aren't going to hurt your ex-wife, are you?" I asked.

"Lauren?" he said. "No. She's welcome to do whatever she likes. I doubt she'd care if I was alive or not."

"Then why did you call her before you died?" I said. "Before you died and came back, I mean?"

"I debated giving her the warning and not you," he said. "I'm starting to wish I had."

"Then why did you decide to stay in town?" I frowned up at him through the darkness. "For that matter, why leave the book in the library even when you knew it would paint targets on our heads? You can't complain that I figured out you were still alive, considering you're the one who left the evidence in our hands in the first place."

"I couldn't very well break into your family's library while there was an active inquiry into my death, could I?" he said. "I hoped you'd figure out I was trying to warn you, but the book's spell was supposed to ensure it didn't give the game away. Henry made certain of it."

"You removed all the instructions on how to undo the curse on the book from your own room, didn't you?" I said. "You've been tampering with the evidence. I suppose your vampire speed made it easy for you to sneak in and out of the hotel without anyone spotting you. But you claim you were trying to warn me when you called the library?"

"Yes, before Henry ruined everything." He scowled. "Not only did he push me to my death, he didn't even have the guts to let me *stay* dead. I know the laws on creating new vampires better than anyone, and I assumed he did, too. Unless he wanted me to take the blame for my own resurrection, of course." He gave a short, bitter laugh.

"Is there a law against creating new vampires, then?" It made sense that Evangeline would want utter control over any new vampires in town, and an ex-vampire hunter would not fare well under her rule. Knowing her, she'd either have him arrested as a rogue or else take revenge on him for all the vampires he'd hunted.

"You're asking someone who hunted rogues for a living," he said. "There's no law against creating new vampires, per se, but all of them are strictly monitored. I don't know whose blood he used to revive me, but I assume he intended for it to seem like I'd deliberately arranged to be turned after I died."

"If he did, then why not let the police deal with it, rather than pushing him out the window?" I said.

"I couldn't leave him alive." He lowered his hood, revealing a face paler than before, with bloodshot eyes under his blond hair. "Not after what he did. I can still remember what it felt like. Death."

Chills raced down my arms. "I saw the Reaper take you into the afterlife himself. What... what did it feel like?"

All I could think of to do was to stall him, keep asking questions until someone found us here.

"Cold." He shuddered. "My career was based on ending lives, not on what comes next."

Yeah, but that's no reason to drag the rest of us into it. I should be terrified, yet after the Grim Reaper, my fear had hit its limit and anger began to creep through. He'd put my family in danger for no good reason, and while he'd ultimately tried to warn us of the danger before his untimely passing, he could have cleared up the case at any time since his return from death and had instead chosen to leave my family in charge of that wretched book.

"Shut up," he said.

I blinked. "I'm sorry, what?"

"Your thoughts are *loud*," he said. "I can't think straight."

Huh? Wait—of course. He must have gained the ability to read minds when he'd woken as a vampire, and I'd bet his years of hunting vampires hadn't prepared him for the reality of *being* one of them. Bloodlust shone in his eyes, and rage, too. Not just at me, but at Henry Blake, for turning him into a vampire and then ditching him. I had to keep him talking, otherwise I'd be the one he took out his rage on.

"I can't control my thoughts," I said. "Look, sooner or later another vampire is going to find you. They'll want to know who created you. And then what?"

His teeth gleamed white and pointed in the darkness. "I'll tell them the truth—that Henry is responsible."

"Telling a witch our plans, are you?" said a voice.

My heartbeat kicked into gear at the sound of Mr Blake entering the room. *He's one, too. A vampire.*

I should have guessed. If it was him who'd turned Mr Spencer, he must have made arrangements in the case of his own death, too. The two of them had been running around in circles trying to outdo one another ever since they'd arrived in town, and now I had two angry vampires to contend with instead of one. Mr Dreyer might not have known what the two of them had done, but he knew they were bad news and had left town while he still could. I didn't blame him a bit.

I'm doomed. I might be miles from Ivory Beach, for all I knew, and my family didn't even know I was missing. Xavier was still under the Grim Reaper's watchful eye, and I had my doubts Evangeline would come to my rescue even if she'd worked out there were two new rogues in town. I hardly believed she hadn't noticed their presence, but then again, they'd hidden their tracks well. I assumed the two of them had enough of their own supplies of blood that they hadn't needed to go hunting yet, but it wouldn't last forever, and I was a living, breathing human.

"You found my trail," said Mr Spencer. "I wondered if you might."

Mr Blake chuckled. "I should have known. You just had to upstage me again, didn't you?"

Trapped between two furious, bloodthirsty vampires. I didn't need to be able to see them squaring up to one another to know I was in real trouble.

15

———

I didn't dare breathe, let alone speak or move. The two vampires faced off, appearing as little more than shadowy outlines of people in the gloom. There was no visible way out except for the door Mr Blake had entered through and if I ran for it, the vampires would catch me in an instant.

I'm going to die here. Both vampires were hungry for blood, and I was the closest source. Even if I stayed put if they stopped fighting for long enough to remember I was here, I was dead.

I felt my way backwards in the hope of finding a way out, and something clinked against my fingers. A small glass bottle, lying on the ground. I didn't need to be able to see its contents to guess it was full of blood. Mr Spencer had prepared well, after all. My hand clenched around the bottle and I rose to my feet, hoping it wasn't empty.

Mr Spencer turned in my direction. "And just where do you think you're going?"

I hurled the bottle into his face, holding my breath. The vampires screamed in unison and fell on one another, unable to resist the smell of blood.

Meanwhile, I backed up to the wall, dug my hand in my pocket and my fingers snagged my Biblio-Witch Inventory. Whipping it out, I tapped the word *light*.

Brightness flooded the room. The vampires let out twin screams of fury and pain, still grappling with one another. I broke into a sprint, reached the wooden door and escaped into the outside world.

I slammed the door behind me. I stood in a field, and judging by the darkness, it was early evening. The house they'd picked looked like more of a shack, bordered by fields on either side with no signs of human habitation. To any normals who ran into me, I'd look like a maniac, dirty and dishevelled, but I didn't care. I had to get away before the vampires caught up with me.

I grabbed my phone from my pocket, but before I could dial, a voice rang out behind me, resonant and clear. "Rory?"

I whirled on the spot, my heart lifting. Xavier walked towards me, his scythe in his hands.

"How'd you find me?" I said.

"I followed you using my Reaper powers," he said. "I heard you talking to my boss and managed to slip away."

I pointed to the house with shaking hands. "The vampires are in there, but I wouldn't get between them."

"Vampires," he said. "Who, exactly?"

"It was Mr Spencer who brought me here," I said. "He and Mr Blake were working together at first, conspiring to lure some rogue vampires to Ivory Beach, but when he got cold feet, they fought and Mr Blake accidentally killed him. Then he tried to undo his mistake…"

"… by turning him into a vampire," said Xavier, his eyes gleaming with understanding. "That explains the blood on the stairs."

"Exactly," I said. "When Mr Spencer woke up, he was raging mad. He pushed Mr Blake out the window, but he must have taken precautions, because he turned into a vampire, too. And now… let's just say they're not best pleased with one another."

A howl echoed from inside the shack and Xavier tensed, his scythe ready. "They're fighting?"

"I threw a bottle of blood at them," I said. "To distract them. I don't know what Mr Spencer planned to do with me, but he didn't want me telling the authorities what he and Mr Blake did. They've been trying to avoid Evangeline, too. If she finds out they're rogues, she won't treat them kindly."

Xavier raised his scythe. "In that case, I'll handle them myself."

As the Reaper reached the door, it bounced off its frame and two figures escaped in twin blurs, resolving into the shadowy forms of the vampires. Both of them were a mess, their faces covered in scratches, eyes wild and bloodshot and fixed accusingly on me.

"Howard might have an issue with harming humans," said Mr Blake, "but I don't. If you don't back off, Reaper, then you'll have to escort your own girlfriend into the afterlife."

Xavier swore. "Keep her out of this. This is your last warning."

Before he could strike, a wave of cold darkness

descended on the field, and even the two vampires went still as the dark shape of the Grim Reaper appeared from the night.

"I wondered what was taking my apprentice so long." His dark gaze landed on the two vampires. "So these are the two rogues, are they?"

"You can't kill us," said Mr Spencer, his voice a terrified squeak. "It's not our time."

"I alone have the right to decide your fates," said the Grim Reaper. "You may have escaped the jaws of death once before, but I own both your souls already."

"Not quite," said Evangeline's voice from behind me. "Those two men are *my* prey."

Oh, no.

Tall and beautiful as ever, the vampires' leader strode towards the Grim Reaper, a scowl forming on her face at the sight of the scythe in his hands.

"I beg to differ," said the Grim Reaper. "These two mortals cheated death. They broke the rules, and they will pay the price."

"They broke *my* laws when they tried to lure rogues into the town to further their own goals," said Evangeline. "Not only that, they are both illegally created vampires, which means they are mine to punish. Their souls returned from death, and that makes them mine, not yours."

The Grim Reaper turned in her direction. "Their souls returned from death through unnatural means, not unlike yours. Do not force me to break my vows."

I tried to catch Xavier's eye, but like me, he stood transfixed, his gaze on his boss squaring up to the vampires' leader. I should have figured that the leader of the vampires and the person responsible for collecting the souls of the dead might have some differences, but not that their animosity might run that deep. No wonder the Grim Reaper had decided to help me, if the alternative was working with Evangeline.

If it came to a conflict between them, the Grim Reaper would surely win, right? He was death personified. Then again, Evangeline herself was deathless. My teeth chattered in my skull. *Get away. Now.*

There was a blur of movement as the two vampires sprinted away across the field, taking the chance to flee for their lives.

Not fast enough. A third blur joined the other two, bright where the others were dark. Xavier halted in between the vampires, and in a swing, his scythe came down.

Darkness spread from his feet across the field, pulling both vampires into its embrace. Behind him appeared the outline of a door edged in light as dazzling as the gleaming sceptre in his hands, and the two vampires began to glow, too. I watched, unable to move or speak, as their ghostly forms floated towards the hovering door at Xavier's back.

The angel of death watched them leave this world, without speaking. When the door had faded along with the rippling shadows behind him, the vampires' bodies were gone.

Then part of the shadows moved. My heart stuttered to a halt as the Grim Reaper stepped into view, looking directly at me. His hood had slipped, revealing a surprisingly human-like face beneath the shadows. His skin was as moon-pale, his eyes as dark blue as the night sky. I broke my gaze from his, hoping fervently he didn't know I'd seen the vampires pass on to the next world.

Then once more, the shadows swept in around him and Xavier, taking the two Reapers away with them.

I released a slow breath. Two ashy heaps lay on the grass, all that remained of the ex-vampire hunters. I was alone, except for…

"Don't look so alarmed," said Evangeline. "You're less than a mile from Ivory Beach, and I'm sure your family will be on their way."

I hope so. My pulse began to race again at the sight of the anger in the vampires' leader's expression, though her eyes showed none of the hunger and rage of the two newly created vampires. Despite that, she was more dangerous than both of them put together.

"I'm disappointed," she said. "You chose to go to the Reaper instead of me."

"I didn't," I said, my throat dry. "Mr Spencer found me first and brought me here. Xavier tracked me, and the Grim Reaper followed his lead."

"Pity. I would have liked to take my time with them." She gave the two piles of ash a disgruntled look. "I suppose this is a fitting punishment, considering how many of my kind they dealt the same fate to."

"They're still dead," I said. "Deader than dead, I mean."

She looked up at me, an inexplicable smile pulling at her mouth. "You have a habit of making dangerous enemies, Aurora Hawthorn."

Does that include you? The thought flickered through my mind before I could stop it. Maybe I hadn't quite got the hang of controlling my thoughts around her after all, but I was exhausted, my nerves frayed from my narrow brush with death, and all I wanted was to go back to the library with my family.

"I make alliances, not enemies," she said. "Though I confess, I did want a look at that book."

"The book is a fake," I told her. "Which you'd have known if you'd read Mr Spencer or Mr Blake's minds."

"Where is the real book?"

"Haven't a clue." It wasn't a lie. I had no doubt that my family would track it down, eventually, but that was a matter for another day. Until I found proof that she wasn't willing to throw my family under the bus the same way those two vampire hunters had, I'd be keeping that book as far from her as possible.

"Pity," said Evangeline.

"Why do you want it, exactly?" I asked. "Because the vampire hunters intended to use it as bait, and only failed because they managed to get one another killed in the process. I don't know about you, but I don't really want any rogues running around town either."

"The book simply interests me, that's all," she said. "I wouldn't dream of putting the town in danger."

I wished Blair, with her lie-sensing powers, could allay my doubts. It was impossible to tell if the vampires' leader was purposefully goading me, or if she did have some sinister motive, but it was abundantly clear Evangeline was out for her own self-interest and nothing else.

"Though I have to say," she added, "I'll be... displeased if you do end up choosing to trust the Grim Reaper over me."

My mouth parted. "You think I trust *him?*"

"I suppose not," she said. "You're an interesting one, Aurora Hawthorn."

I didn't know what to say to that, so I kept silent.

"Oh, look." She pointed to several red-haired figures approaching. "I'm right. There's your family."

Sure enough, there they were. Aunt Adelaide, Aunt Candace, Estelle… even Cass. They'd come to find me.

It was time to go home.

16

The following morning, we got rid of the book.

I entered the library's lobby to find my family members gathering around a sealed package lying on the front desk. Muffled screaming came from within, but it stilled when Cass gave it a jab with her wand.

Sylvester extended a foot and prodded the sealed package. "Are you sure you don't want me to drop it into the sea?"

"That wouldn't be fair on the marine life in the ocean," Cass said. "Post it to the vampires instead."

"No thanks," I said. "We're lucky no rogues did come to town, considering how those two vampire hunters would sooner have fought one another rather than do any actual vampire hunting."

"I have other people I'd like to send it to," remarked Aunt Candace.

"No, you don't," said Estelle. "Aunt Candace, you can't post it to a friend of yours. Not this time."

"I can think of a few people who deserve it." She gave a rather evil chuckle. "Don't look at me like that, Adelaide, I'm not going to. But I see nothing wrong with sending those rogue vampires on a wild phoenix chase. By the time word gets out that the book's not the genuine article, they should be miles away from town."

"She has a point," I said. "Do you think the vampires are still after it, then?"

"I don't doubt they are," said Aunt Adelaide. "I think we'll send the book somewhere up north. How does Scotland sound?"

"Excellent." Aunt Candace clapped her hands. "We'll tell everyone we know that the book is being shipped north. Meanwhile, we'll have it destroyed."

"Of course." Aunt Adelaide walked towards the desk. "I trust you can ensure it reaches its destination, Sylvester?"

"What?" said the owl. "Oh, all *right*. Fine. But you'd better make sure no vampires come on my tail."

"Of course." Aunt Adelaide followed the owl out of the library. "Just make sure everyone sees you flying north, and then we'll take off the sentience spell and destroy it."

"The animals knew," said Cass. "That the book was a fake, I mean. They were spooked from the instant Rory brought it in here."

"Hey, it wasn't Rory's fault," said Estelle.

"Never said it was."

"You implied it." Estelle gave an eye-roll. "Cass, are you even trying to turn over a new leaf?"

"Whoever said I had to?" she said. "We both know Rory only brought the book back here to begin with because she didn't want the whole world to hear her wish for the Reaper to come back."

How did she know that? For someone who pretended not to care about anyone, Cass could be amazingly perceptive.

Then she added, "Though he did ditch you last night, so perhaps not."

"Cass!" said Estelle. "When the Grim Reaper asks you to go somewhere, you don't have a choice, even if you're his apprentice. Right, Rory?"

"You bet." Cass wouldn't be Cass without the occasional snide comment. Anyway, she was only looking out for the library. And for her pets. Mostly the pets. "What did *you* wish for, anyway?"

"None of your business," she said.

"Please say it wasn't a unicorn," said Estelle. "As for me, I wished I could hand in my thesis in one piece."

Cass snorted. "Now I know why you two get on so well. You're the only two people in existence who get excited about going back to school."

At that moment, Jet flew over and landed on my shoulder. "Your friend is here!" he squeaked. "The bad book is gone!"

"Yes, it is." I made my way over to the front desk, where Blair waved at me from beside the front door.

"Hey," she said. "I just came to say bye. And to thank you again for your help."

"No problem," I said. "Thanks for helping me with that book. Sorry it was so much trouble."

"I've dealt with worse," she said. "Nice meeting you, Jet," she added, as my familiar flew over to greet her. "Where is the talking book, anyway?"

"Gone," I said. "Well, it's on the way out. In fact, Jet, I need you to do me a favour."

"Of course!" he squeaked.

"We need to put out the word that the book is heading north," I said. "That way, if there are any vampires looking for it, they won't come here. Tell everyone you see it's going to Scotland. Can you do that?"

"I'll tell everyone!" he promised, taking flight.

Blair grinned. "Good job there. We can spread the word, too, on our way back."

"Thanks," I said. "Have a safe trip home."

"I will. And thank you for showing me around the library." Blair waved goodbye, pushing open the door.

"Miaow," said a voice at her feet.

I looked down to see Sky sitting beside the desk. Once again, he'd entered without my noticing. Underneath his extended front paw lay the trapdoor leading into the vampire's basement.

Wait…

"You left the trapdoor open?" I frowned at the little black cat. "You mean you knew… you knew I needed to see the vampire?"

"Miaow," he said.

Then he sauntered towards the door and vanished after his owner.

Was that normal for magical cats? I hadn't a clue.

I was about to return to work when the door opened again, and Xavier walked in. "Hey, Rory."

"Hey." I smiled at him. "I just said goodbye to Blair."

"I saw her on the way out," he said. "She got whatever she needed from the library, then?"

"She did," I said. "She and Nathan are heading back home today. The book's on its way north, too. Well, that's what we're telling everyone."

"Oh, so that's what your familiar's flying around telling people in the town square," he said.

"I did tell him to spread the word. Figured it was the best way."

"You aren't wrong." He drew in a breath. "Come out with me tonight."

I startled. "What? You mean on a date?"

"Sure."

I blinked a couple of times, nonplussed. The note on which the Grim Reaper had left us yesterday hadn't exactly prepared me for him to ask me out in such a direct manner. "Are you certain?"

"I am." He stepped towards the door. "I'll pick you up at seven."

"I'll be there."

———

That evening, Xavier and I walked out into the cold night air. A companionable silence drifted over us, but I couldn't quell the flow of questions rising in my mind. Finally, I turned to him.

"Are you interested in me?" I asked. "Or not?"

"I am," he said. "I'm sorry for leaving town. I'm also sorry for how my boss treated you. I didn't know he'd go so far as to leave you threatening notes. I talked to him about it."

"But...?" I could read between the lines. He was interested, but as long as he was the Reaper, dating a human wasn't an option. It never had been. This was just his way of letting me down gently.

Yet he still didn't let go of my hand as we walked.

Okay. Maybe the Grim Reaper isn't okay with this, but Xavier is, and that's what's important, isn't it?

I stilled as we reached the seafront. A shadow shaped like a person stood waiting for us, blocking my view of the night sky. I'd expected it, on some level, but my heart still plummeted at the sight of the Grim Reaper.

"Don't worry," Xavier whispered. "I won't let him harm you. He just wants a word with you."

I did my best to school my expression into blankness and approached his shadowy form.

"Grim Reaper." I didn't know how else to address him.

"Aurora."

We remained silent for a long moment while I waited for him to speak.

"You are... vexing," said the Grim Reaper. "You shouldn't have gone after those vampires alone."

"I didn't," I said. "They captured me, and I didn't have any way to call for help. Not from you or Xavier, anyway."

"You've seen things that humans shouldn't see," he went on.

"It wasn't exactly a choice."

"You seem to have made an enemy of some dangerous people, too," he added, as though I hadn't spoken. "The group of vampires you encountered have been causing issues for the Reapers for some time."

"Wait... they have?" Xavier hadn't said so, but it was clear the Grim Reaper didn't tell him everything, either.

His gaze went to the library, visible above the town square. "Your family provides a valuable service to the town, but your interest in my apprentice is causing me no end of trouble. He's even more distracted when he *doesn't* have contact with you, and it's not good for his position as Reaper."

Wait, he is? I risked a glance at Xavier, but the Grim Reaper's shadows blocked him from view.

"I'm not going to monopolise Xavier's attention," I said. "I have a job, too. I have friends and family as well. If he's happier with me in his life, it's advantageous for both of you to let us keep in touch, right?"

"Reapers shouldn't have friends."

"It's not doing any harm," I said. "Xavier doesn't want to quit being the Reaper and he doesn't want to give me up, either. The two aren't mutually exclusive. Besides, you said yourself… he's better at his job when he's allowed contact with me. What's wrong with a compromise?"

The shadows lifted a little, revealing the Grim Reaper's real face. He *had* been human once, I was sure.

"Xavier is young for a Reaper apprentice," he said. "Young enough to let his emotions get the better of him. Perhaps I will allow him this… flirtation."

My heart missed a beat. "You mean you'll let us date one another?"

"Until he comes to his senses," he said. "Is that good enough for you?"

Maybe if I'd been the person I'd been when I first moved to town, I would have said yes.

As it was… "No."

"Excuse me?" said the Grim Reaper. Beneath the chilling resonance of his voice, there was a hint of genuine surprise.

"I don't want you to give him permission to date me and then take it back later. Or drag him out of town and leave threatening messages for me without his knowledge. I want a guarantee that you'll let anything to do with our relationship stay between the two of us only." I took in a deep breath. "That's all."

For a moment, I expected him to get out his scythe, but he merely turned away. "Then I will respect your wishes, provided you respect mine. Do not distract him from his duties."

"I won't." *Within reason.* For instance, I wouldn't say no to taking him for a proper date tonight, without any vampires or screaming books involved.

The shadows folded in, and the next second, he was gone. I released a slow breath. I'd gambled and won against the Grim Reaper, and now Xavier and I would be free to pursue a relationship without the shadow of his disapproval hanging over our heads.

Xavier stepped to my side. "That was risky."

"It was worth it." I grinned. "I thought about asking him to let you have a mobile phone, too, but that can wait for next time."

His arms came around me, and he kissed me under the darkening sky. Only when he let go of me did I look up, breathless, at the blanket of stars above.

Maybe I'd get my wish after all.

ABOUT THE AUTHOR

Elle Adams lives in the middle of England, where she spends most of her time reading an ever-growing mountain of books, planning her next adventure, or writing. Elle's books are humorous mysteries with a paranormal twist, packed with magical mayhem.

She also writes urban and contemporary fantasy novels as Emma L. Adams.

Find Elle on Facebook at https://www.facebook.com/pg/ElleAdamsAuthor/